PENGUIN BOOKS

Trickery

Roald Dahl is best known for his mischievous, wildly inventive stories for children. But throughout his life he was also a prolific and acclaimed writer of stories for adults. These sinister, surprising tales continue to entertain, amuse and shock generations of readers even today.

Trickery

ROALD DAHL

PENGUIN BOOKS

PENGUIN BOOKS

UK | USA | Canada | Ireland | Australia
India | New Zealand | South Africa

Penguin Books is part of the Penguin Random House group of companies
whose addresses can be found at global.penguinrandomhouse.com.

These stories have been previously published in a variety of publications.
Details of each story's original publication are provided at the start of each
chapter and constitute an extension of this copyright page.
This collection first published in Penguin Books 2017
001

Set in 12.5/14.75 pt Garamond MT Std
Typeset by Jouve (UK), Milton Keynes
Printed in Great Britain by Clays Ltd, St Ives plc

A CIP catalogue record for this book is available from the British Library

ISBN: 978–1–405–93323–0

Contents

The Wish

First published in *Someone Like You* (1953)

Under the palm of one hand the child became aware of the scab of an old cut on his knee-cap. He bent forward to examine it closely. A scab was always a fascinating thing; it presented a special challenge he was never able to resist.

Yes, he thought, I will pick it off, even if it isn't ready, even if the middle of it sticks, even if it hurts like anything.

With a fingernail he began to explore cautiously around the edges of the scab. He got the nail underneath it, and when he raised it, but ever so slightly, it suddenly came off, the whole hard brown scab came off beautifully, leaving an interesting little circle of smooth red skin.

Nice. Very nice indeed. He rubbed the circle and it didn't hurt. He picked up the scab, put it on his thigh and flipped it with a finger so that it flew away and landed on the edge of the carpet, the enormous red and black and yellow carpet that stretched the whole length of the hall from the stairs on which he sat to the front door in the distance. A tremendous carpet. Bigger than the tennis lawn. Much bigger than that. He regarded it gravely, settling his eyes upon it with mild pleasure. He had never really noticed it before, but now, all of a sudden, the colours seemed to brighten mysteriously and spring out at him in a most dazzling way.

You see, he told himself, I know how it is. The red parts of the carpet are red-hot lumps of coal. What I must do is this: I must walk all the way along it to the front door without touching them. If I touch the red I will be burned. As a matter of fact, I will be burned up completely. And the black parts of the carpet . . . yes, the black parts are snakes, poisonous snakes, adders mostly, and cobras, thick like tree-trunks round the middle, and if I touch one of *them*, I'll be bitten and I'll die before teatime. And if I get across safely, without being burned and without being bitten, I will be given a puppy for my birthday tomorrow.

He got to his feet and climbed higher up the stairs to obtain a better view of this vast tapestry of colour and death. Was it possible? Was there enough yellow? Yellow was the only colour he was allowed to walk on. Could it be done? This was not a journey to be undertaken lightly; the risks were too great for that. The child's face – a fringe of white-gold hair, two large blue eyes, a small pointed chin – peered down anxiously over the banisters. The yellow was a bit thin in places and there were one or two widish gaps, but it did seem to go all the way along to the other end. For someone who had only yesterday triumphantly travelled the whole length of the brick path from the stables to the summer-house without touching the cracks, this carpet thing should not be too difficult. Except for the snakes. The mere thought of snakes sent a fine electricity of fear running like pins down the backs of his legs and under the soles of his feet.

He came slowly down the stairs and advanced to the edge of the carpet. He extended one small sandalled foot and placed it cautiously upon a patch of yellow. Then he brought the other foot up, and there was just enough room for him to stand with the two feet together. There! He had started! His bright oval face was curiously intent, a shade whiter perhaps than before, and he was holding his arms out sideways to assist his balance. He took another step, lifting his foot high over a patch of black, aiming carefully with his toe for a narrow channel of yellow on the other side. When he had completed the second step he paused to rest, standing very stiff and still. The narrow channel of yellow ran forward unbroken for at least five yards and he advanced gingerly along it, bit by bit, as though walking a tightrope. Where it finally curled off sideways, he had to take another long stride, this time over a vicious-looking mixture of black and red. Halfway across he began to wobble. He waved his arms around wildly, windmill fashion, to keep his balance, and he got across safely and rested again on the other side. He was quite breathless now, and so tense he stood high on his toes all the time, arms out sideways, fists clenched. He was on a big safe island of yellow. There was lots of room on it, he couldn't possibly fall off, and he stood there resting, hesitating, waiting, wishing he could stay for ever on this big safe yellow island. But the fear of not getting the puppy compelled him to go on.

Step by step, he edged farther ahead, and between each one he paused to decide exactly where next he should put his foot. Once, he had a choice of ways, either to left or right, and he chose the left because although it seemed the more difficult, there was not so much black in that direction. The black was what made him nervous. He glanced quickly over his shoulder to see how far he had come. Nearly halfway. There could be no turning back now. He was in the middle and he couldn't turn back and he couldn't jump off sideways either because it was too far, and when he looked at all the red and all the black that lay ahead of him, he felt that old sudden sickening surge of panic in his chest – like last Easter-time, that afternoon when he got lost all alone in the darkest part of Piper's Wood.

He took another step, placing his foot carefully upon the only little piece of yellow within reach, and this time the point of the foot came within a centimetre of some black. It wasn't touching the black, he could see it wasn't touching, he could see the small line of yellow separating the toe of his sandal from the black; but the snake stirred as though sensing the nearness, and raised its head and gazed at the foot with bright beady eyes, watching to see if it was going to touch.

'*I'm not touching you! You mustn't bite me! You know I'm not touching you!*'

Another snake slid up noiselessly beside the first, raised its head, two heads now, two pairs of eyes staring at the foot, gazing at a little naked place just below the sandal strap where the skin showed through. The child went high up on his toes and stayed there, frozen stiff with terror. It was minutes before he dared to move again.

The next step would have to be a really long one. There was this deep curling river of black that ran clear across the width of the carpet, and he was forced by this position to cross it at its widest part. He thought first of trying to jump it, but decided he couldn't be sure of landing accurately on the narrow band of yellow the other side. He took a deep breath, lifted one foot, and inch by inch he pushed it out in front of him, far far out, then down and down until at last the tip of his sandal was across and resting safely on the edge of the yellow. He leaned forward, transferring his weight to his front foot. Then he tried to bring the back foot up as well. He strained and pulled and jerked his body, but the legs were too wide apart and he couldn't make it. He tried to get back again. He couldn't do that either. He was doing the splits and he was properly stuck. He glanced down and saw this deep curling river of black underneath him. Parts of it were stirring now, and uncoiling and sliding and beginning to shine with a dreadfully oily glister. He wobbled, waved his arms frantically to keep his balance, but that seemed to make it worse. He was starting to go over. He was going over to the right, quite slowly he was going over, then faster and faster, and at the last moment, instinctively he put out a hand to break the fall and the next thing he saw was this bare hand of his going right into the middle of a great glistening mass of black and he gave one piercing cry of terror as it touched.

Outside in the sunshine, far away behind the house, the mother was looking for her son.

Beware of the Dog

First published in *Harper's* (October 1944)

Down below there was only a vast white undulating sea of cloud. Above there was the sun, and the sun was white like the clouds, because it is never yellow when one looks at it from high in the air.

He was still flying the Spitfire. His right hand was on the stick and he was working the rudder bar with his left leg alone. It was quite easy. The machine was flying well. He knew what he was doing.

Everything is fine, he thought. I'm doing all right. I'm doing nicely. I know my way home. I'll be there in half an hour. When I land I shall taxi in and switch off my engine and I shall say, Help me to get out, will you. I shall make my voice sound ordinary and natural and none of them will take any notice. Then I shall say, Someone help me to get out. I can't do it alone because I've lost one of my legs. They'll all laugh and think that I'm joking and I shall say, All right, come and have a look, you unbelieving bastards. Then Yorky will climb up on to the wing and look inside. He'll probably be sick because of all the blood and the mess. I shall laugh and say, For God's sake, help me get out.

He glanced down again at his right leg. There was not much of it left. The cannon-shell had taken him on the thigh, just above the knee, and now there was nothing but a great mess and a lot of blood. But there was no pain. When he looked down, he felt as though he were seeing something that did not belong to him. It had nothing to do with him. It was just a mess which happened to be there in the cockpit; something strange and unusual and rather interesting. It was like finding a dead cat on the sofa.

He really felt fine, and because he still felt fine, he felt excited and unafraid.

I won't even bother to call up on the radio for the blood-wagon, he thought. It isn't necessary. And when I land I'll sit there quite normally and say, Some of you fellows come and help me out, will you, because I've lost one of my legs. That will be funny. I'll laugh a little while I'm saying it; I'll say it calmly and slowly, and they'll think I'm joking. When Yorky comes up on to the wing and gets sick, I'll say, Yorky, you old son of a bitch, have you fixed my car yet? Then when I get out I'll make my report. Later I'll go up to London. I'll take that half bottle of whisky with me and I'll give it to Bluey. We'll sit in her room and drink it. I'll get the water out of the bathroom tap. I won't say much until it's time to go to bed, then I'll say, Bluey I've got a surprise for you. I lost a leg today. But I don't mind so long as you don't. It doesn't even hurt. We'll go everywhere in cars. I always hated walking except when I walked down the street of the coppersmiths in Baghdad, but I could go in a rickshaw. I could go home and chop wood, but the head always flies off the axe. Hot water, that's what it needs; put it in the bath and make the handle swell. I chopped lots of wood last time I went home and I put the axe in the bath . . .

Then he saw the sun shining on the engine cowling of his machine. He saw the sun shining on the rivets in the metal, and he remembered the aeroplane and he remembered where he was. He realized that he was no longer feeling good; that he was sick and giddy. His head kept falling forward on to his chest because his neck seemed no longer to have any strength. But he knew that he was flying the Spitfire. He could feel the handle of the stick between the fingers of his right hand.

I'm going to pass out, he thought. Any moment now I'm going to pass out.

He looked at his altimeter. Twenty-one thousand. To test himself he tried to read the hundreds as well as the thousands. Twenty-one thousand and what? As he looked the dial became blurred and he could not even see the needle. He knew then that he must bale out; that there was not a second to lose, otherwise he would become unconscious. Quickly, frantically, he tried to slide back the hood with his left hand, but he had not the strength. For a second he took his right hand off the stick and with both hands he managed to push the hood back. The rush of cold air on his face seemed to help. He had a moment of great clearness. His actions became orderly and precise. That is what happens with a good pilot. He took some quick deep breaths from his oxygen mask, and as he did so, he looked out over the side of the cockpit. Down below there was only a vast white sea of cloud and he realized that he did not know where he was.

It'll be the Channel, he thought. I'm sure to fall in the drink.

He throttled back, pulled off his helmet, undid his straps and pushed the stick hard over to the left. The Spitfire dipped its port wing and turned smoothly over on to its back. The pilot fell out.

As he fell, he opened his eyes, because he knew that he must not pass out before he had pulled the cord. On one side he saw the sun; on the other he saw the whiteness of the clouds, and as he fell, as he somersaulted in the air, the white clouds chased the sun and the sun chased the clouds. They chased each other in a small circle; they ran faster and faster and there was the sun and the clouds and the clouds and the sun, and the clouds came nearer until suddenly there was no longer any sun but only a great whiteness. The whole world was white and there was nothing in it. It was so white that sometimes it looked black, and after a time it was either white or black, but mostly it was white. He watched it as it turned from white to black, then back to white again, and the white stayed for a long time, but the black lasted only for a few seconds. He got into the habit of going to sleep during the white periods, of waking up just in time to see the world when it was black. The black was very quick. Sometimes it was only a flash, a flash of black lightning. The white was slow and in the slowness of it, he always dozed off.

One day, when it was white, he put out a hand and he touched something. He took it between his fingers and crumpled it. For a time he lay there, idly letting the tips of his fingers play with the thing which they had touched. Then slowly he opened his eyes, looked down at his hand and saw that he was holding something which was white.

It was the edge of a sheet. He knew it was a sheet because he could see the texture of the material and the stitchings on the hem. He screwed up his eyes and opened them again quickly. This time he saw the room. He saw the bed in which he was lying: he saw the grey walls and the door and the green curtains over the window. There were some roses on the table by his bed.

Then he saw the basin on the table near the roses. It was a white enamel basin and beside it there was a small medicine glass.

This is a hospital, he thought. I am in a hospital. But he could remember nothing. He lay back on his pillow, looking at the ceiling and wondering what had happened. He was gazing at the smooth greyness of the ceiling which was so clean and grey, and then suddenly he saw a fly walking upon it. The sight of this fly, the suddenness of seeing this small black speck on a sea of grey, brushed the surface of his brain, and quickly, in that second, he remembered everything. He remembered the Spitfire and he remembered the altimeter showing twenty-one thousand feet. He remembered the pushing back of the hood with both hands and he remembered the baling out. He remembered his leg.

It seemed all right now. He looked down at the end of the bed, but he could not tell. He put one hand underneath the bedclothes and felt for his knees. He found one of them, but when he felt for the other, his hand touched something which was soft and covered in bandages.

Just then the door opened and a nurse came in.

'Hello,' she said. 'So you've waked up at last.'

She was not good-looking, but she was large and clean. She was between thirty and forty and she had fair hair. More than that he did not notice.

'Where am I?'

'You're a lucky fellow. You landed in a wood near the beach. You're in Brighton. They brought you in two days ago, and now you're all fixed up. You look fine.'

'I've lost a leg,' he said.

'That's nothing. We'll get you another one. Now you must go to sleep. The doctor will be coming to see you in about an hour.' She picked up the basin and the medicine glass and went out.

But he did not sleep. He wanted to keep his eyes open because he was frightened that if he shut them again everything would go away. He lay looking at the ceiling. The fly was still there. It was very energetic. It would run forward very fast for a few inches, then it would stop. Then it would run forward again, stop, run forward, and every now and then it would take off and buzz around viciously in small circles. It always landed back in the same place on the ceiling and started running and stopping all over again. He watched it for so long that after a while it was no longer a fly, but only a black speck upon a sea of grey, and he was still watching it when the nurse opened the door, and stood aside while the doctor came in. He was an Army doctor, a major, and he had some last-war ribbons on his chest. He was bald and small, but he had a cheerful face and kind eyes.

'Well, well,' he said. 'So you've decided to wake up at last. How are you feeling?'

'I feel all right.'

'That's the stuff. You'll be up and about in no time.'

The doctor took his wrist to feel his pulse.

'By the way,' he said, 'some of the lads from your squadron were ringing up and asking about you. They wanted to come along and see you, but I said that they'd better wait a day or two. Told them you were all right and that they could come and see you a little later on. Just lie quiet and take it easy for a bit. Got something to read?' He glanced at the table with the roses. 'No. Well, Nurse will look after you. She'll get you anything you want. With that he waved his hand and went out, followed by the large clean nurse.

When they had gone, he lay back and looked at the ceiling again. The fly was still there and as he lay watching it he heard the noise of an aeroplane in the distance. He lay listening to the sound of its engines. It was a long way away. I wonder what it is, he thought. Let me see if I can place it. Suddenly he jerked his head sharply to one side. Anyone who has been bombed can tell the noise of a Junkers 88. They can tell most other German bombers for that matter, but especially a Junkers 88. The engines seem to sing a duet. There is a deep vibrating bass voice and with it there is a high-pitched tenor. It is the singing of the tenor which makes the sound of a Ju-88 something which one cannot mistake.

He lay listening to the noise and he felt quite certain about what it was. But where were the sirens and where the guns? That German pilot certainly had a nerve coming near Brighton alone in daylight.

The aircraft was always far away and soon the noise

faded away into the distance. Later on there was another. This one, too, was far away, but there was the same deep undulating bass and the high swinging tenor and there was no mistaking it. He had heard that noise every day during the Battle.

He was puzzled. There was a bell on the table by the bed. He reached out his hand and rang it. He heard the noise of footsteps down the corridor. The nurse came in.

'Nurse, what were those aeroplanes?'

'I'm sure I don't know. I didn't hear them. Probably fighters or bombers. I expect they were returning from France. Why, what's the matter?'

'They were Ju-88s. I'm sure they were Ju-88s. I know the sound of the engines. There were two of them. What were they doing over here?'

The nurse came up to the side of his bed and began to straighten out the sheets and tuck them in under the mattress.

'Gracious me, what things you imagine. You mustn't worry about a thing like that. Would you like me to get you something to read?'

'No, thank you.'

She patted his pillow and brushed back the hair from his forehead with her hand.

'They never come over in daylight any longer. You know that. They were probably Lancasters or Flying Fortresses.'

'Nurse.'

'Yes.'

'Could I have a cigarette?'

'Why certainly you can.'

She went out and came back almost at once with a packet of Players and some matches. She handed one to him and when he had put it in his mouth, she struck a match and lit it.

'If you want me again,' she said, 'just ring the bell,' and she went out.

Once towards evening he heard the noise of another aircraft. It was far away, but even so he knew that it was a single-engined machine. It was going fast; he could tell that. He could not place it. It wasn't a Spit, and it wasn't a Hurricane. It did not sound like an American engine either. They make more noise. He did not know what it was, and it worried him greatly. Perhaps I am very ill, he thought. Perhaps I am imagining things. Perhaps I am a little delirious. I simply do not know what to think.

That evening the nurse came in with a basin of hot water and began to wash him.

'Well,' she said, 'I hope you don't think that we're being bombed.'

She had taken off his pyjama top and was soaping his right arm with a flannel. He did not answer.

She rinsed the flannel in the water, rubbed more soap on it, and began to wash his chest.

'You're looking fine this evening,' she said. 'They operated on you as soon as you came in. They did a marvellous job. You'll be all right. I've got a brother in the RAF,' she added. 'Flying bombers.'

He said, 'I went to school in Brighton.'

She looked up quickly. 'Well, that's fine,' she said. 'I expect you'll know some people in the town.'

'Yes,' he said, 'I know quite a few.'

She had finished washing his chest and arms. Now she turned back the bedclothes so that his left leg was uncovered. She did it in such a way that his bandaged stump remained under the sheets. She undid the cord of his pyjama trousers and took them off. There was no trouble because they had cut off the right trouser-leg so that it could not interfere with the bandages. She began to wash his left leg and the rest of his body. This was the first time he had had a bed-bath and he was embarrassed. She laid a towel under his leg and began washing his foot with the flannel. She said, 'This wretched soap won't lather at all. It's the water. It's as hard as nails.'

He said, 'None of the soap is very good now and, of course, with hard water it's hopeless.' As he said it he remembered something. He remembered the baths which he used to take at school in Brighton, in the long stone-floored bathroom which had four baths in a row. He remembered how the water was so soft that you had to take a shower afterwards to get all the soap off your body, and he remembered how the foam used to float on the surface of the water, so that you could not see your legs underneath. He remembered that sometimes they were given calcium tablets because the school doctor used to say that soft water was bad for the teeth.

'In Brighton,' he said, 'the water isn't . . .'

He did not finish the sentence. Something had occurred to him; something so fantastic and absurd that for a moment he felt like telling the nurse about it and having a good laugh.

She looked up. 'The water isn't what?' she said.

'Nothing,' he answered. 'I was dreaming.'

She rinsed the flannel in the basin, wiped the soap off his leg and dried him with a towel.

'It's nice to be washed,' he said. 'I feel better.' He was feeling his face with his hand. 'I need a shave.'

'We'll do that tomorrow,' she said. 'Perhaps you can do it yourself then.'

That night he could not sleep. He lay awake thinking of the Junkers 88s and of the hardness of the water. He could think of nothing else. They were Ju-88s, he said to himself. I know they were. And yet it is not possible, because they would not be flying around so low over here in broad daylight. I know that it is true and yet I know that it is impossible. Perhaps I am ill. Perhaps I am behaving like a fool and do not know what I am doing or saying. Perhaps I am delirious. For a long time he lay awake thinking these things, and once he sat up in bed and said aloud, 'I will prove that I am not crazy. I will make a little speech about something complicated and intellectual. I will talk about what to do with Germany after the war.' But before he had time to begin, he was asleep.

He woke just as the first light of day was showing through the slit in the curtains over the window. The room was still dark, but he could tell that it was already beginning to get light outside. He lay looking at the grey light which was showing through the slit in the curtain and as he lay there he remembered the day before. He remembered the Junkers 88s and the hardness of the water; he remembered the large pleasant nurse and the kind doctor, and now a small grain of doubt took root in his mind and it began to grow.

He looked around the room. The nurse had taken the roses out the night before. There was nothing except the table with a packet of cigarettes, a box of matches and an ashtray. The room was bare. It was no longer warm or friendly. It was not even comfortable. It was cold and empty and very quiet.

Slowly the grain of doubt grew, and with it came fear, a light, dancing fear that warned but did not frighten; the kind of fear that one gets not because one is afraid, but because one feels that there is something wrong. Quickly the doubt and the fear grew so that he became restless and angry, and when he touched his forehead with his hand, he found that it was damp with sweat. He knew then that he must do something; that he must find some way of proving to himself that he was either right or wrong, and he looked up and saw again the window and the green curtains. From where he lay, that window was right in front of him, but it was fully ten yards away. Somehow he must reach it and look out. The idea became an obsession with him and soon he could think of nothing except the window. But what about his leg? He put his hand underneath the bedclothes and felt the thick bandaged stump which was all that was left on the right-hand side. It seemed all right. It didn't hurt. But it would not be easy.

He sat up. Then he pushed the bedclothes aside and put his left leg on the floor. Slowly, carefully, he swung his body over until he had both hands on the floor as well;

then he was out of bed, kneeling on the carpet. He looked at the stump. It was very short and thick, covered with bandages. It was beginning to hurt and he could feel it throbbing. He wanted to collapse, lie down on the carpet and do nothing, but he knew that he must go on.

With two arms and one leg, he crawled over towards the window. He would reach forward as far as he could with his arms, then he would give a little jump and slide his left leg along after them. Each time he did it, it jarred his wound so that he gave a soft grunt of pain, but he continued to crawl across the floor on two hands and one knee. When he got to the window he reached up, and one at a time he placed both hands on the sill. Slowly he raised himself up until he was standing on his left leg. Then quickly he pushed aside the curtains and looked out.

He saw a small house with a grey tiled roof standing alone beside a narrow lane, and immediately behind it there was a ploughed field. In front of the house there was an untidy garden, and there was a green hedge separating the garden from the lane. He was looking at the hedge when he saw the sign. It was just a piece of board nailed to the top of a short pole, and because the hedge had not been trimmed for a long time, the branches had grown out around the sign so that it seemed almost as though it had been placed in the middle of the hedge. There was something written on the board with white paint. He pressed his head against the glass of the window, trying to read what it said. The first letter was a G, he could see that. The second was an A, and the third was an R. One after another he managed to see what the letters were. There were three words, and slowly he spelled the letters out aloud to himself as he managed to read them. G-A-R-D-E A-U C-H-I-E-N, *Garde au chien.* That is what it said.

He stood there balancing on one leg and holding tightly to the edges of the window sill with his hands, staring at the sign and at the whitewashed lettering of the words. For a moment he could think of nothing at all. He stood there looking at the sign, repeating the words over and over to himself. Slowly he began to realize the full meaning of the thing. He looked up at the cottage and at the ploughed field. He looked at the small orchard on the left of the cottage and he looked at the green countryside beyond. 'So this is France,' he said. 'I am in France.'

Now the throbbing in his right thigh was very great. It felt as though someone was pounding the end of his stump with a hammer and suddenly the pain became so intense that it affected his head. For a moment he thought he was going to fall. Quickly he knelt down again, crawled back to the bed and hoisted himself in. He pulled the bedclothes over himself and lay back on the pillow, exhausted. He could still think of nothing at all except the small sign by the hedge and the ploughed field and the orchard. It was the words on the sign that he could not forget.

It was some time before the nurse came in. She came carrying a basin of hot water and she said, 'Good morning, how are you today?'

He said, 'Good morning, Nurse.'

The pain was still great under the bandages, but he did

not wish to tell this woman anything. He looked at her as she busied herself with getting the washing things ready. He looked at her more carefully now. Her hair was very fair. She was tall and big-boned and her face seemed pleasant. But there was something a little uneasy about her eyes. They were never still. They never looked at anything for more than a moment and they moved too quickly from one place to another in the room. There was something about her movements also. They were too sharp and nervous to go well with the casual manner in which she spoke.

She set down the basin, took off his pyjama top and began to wash him.

'Did you sleep well?'

'Yes.'

'Good,' she said. She was washing his arms and his chest.

'I believe there's someone coming down to see you from the Air Ministry after breakfast,' she went on. 'They want a report or something. I expect you know all about it. How you got shot down and all that. I won't let him stay long, so don't worry.'

He did not answer. She finished washing him and gave him a toothbrush and some toothpowder. He brushed his teeth, rinsed his mouth and spat the water out into the basin.

Later she brought him his breakfast on a tray, but he did not want to eat. He was still feeling weak and sick and he wished only to lie still and think about what had happened. And there was a sentence running through his head. It was a sentence which Johnny, the intelligence officer of his squadron, always repeated to the pilots every day before they went out. He could see Johnny now, leaning against the wall of the dispersal hut with his pipe in his hand, saying, 'And if they get you, don't forget, just your name, rank and number. Nothing else. For God's sake, say nothing else.'

'There you are,' she said as she put the tray on his lap. 'I've got you an egg. Can you manage all right?'

'Yes.'

She stood beside the bed. 'Are you feeling all right?'

'Yes.'

'Good. If you want another egg I might be able to get you one.'

'This is all right.'

'Well, just ring the bell if you want any more.' And she went out.

He had just finished eating, when the nurse came in again.

She said, 'Wing Commander Roberts is here. I've told him that he can only stay for a few minutes.'

She beckoned with her hand and the wing commander came in.

'Sorry to bother you like this,' he said.

He was an ordinary RAF officer, dressed in a uniform which was a little shabby. He wore wings and a DFC. He was fairly tall and thin with plenty of black hair. His teeth, which were irregular and widely spaced, stuck out a little even when he closed his mouth. As he spoke he took a printed form and a pencil from his pocket and he pulled up a chair and sat down.

'How are you feeling?'

There was no answer.

'Tough luck about your leg. I know how you feel. I hear you put up a fine show before they got you.'

The man in the bed was lying quite still, watching the man in the chair.

The man in the chair said, 'Well, let's get this stuff over. I'm afraid you'll have to answer a few questions so that I can fill in this combat report. Let me see now, first of all, what was your squadron?'

The man in the bed did not move. He looked straight at the wing commander and he said, 'My name is Peter Williamson, my rank is squadron leader and my number is nine seven two four five seven.'

The Champion of the World

First published in the *New Yorker*,
31 January 1959

All day, in between serving customers, we had been crouching over the table in the office of the filling-station, preparing the raisins. They were plump and soft and swollen from being soaked in water, and when you nicked them with a razor-blade the skin sprang open and the jelly stuff inside squeezed out as easily as you could wish.

But we had a hundred and ninety-six of them to do altogether and the evening was nearly upon us before we had finished.

'Don't they look marvellous!' Claud cried, rubbing his hands together hard. 'What time is it, Gordon?'

'Just after five.'

Through the window we could see a station-wagon pulling up at the pumps with a woman at the wheel and about eight children in the back eating ice-creams.

'We ought to be moving soon,' Claud said. 'The whole thing'll be a washout if we don't arrive before sunset, you realize that.' He was getting twitchy now. His face had the same flushed and pop-eyed look it got before a dog-race or when there was a date with Clarice in the evening.

We both went outside and Claud gave the woman the number of gallons she wanted. When she had gone, he remained standing in the middle of the driveway squinting anxiously up at the sun which was now only the width of a man's hand above the line of trees along the crest of the ridge on the far side of the valley.

'All right,' I said. 'Lock up.'

He went quickly from pump to pump, securing each nozzle in its holder with a small padlock.

'You'd better take off that yellow pullover,' he said.

'Why should I?'

'You'll be shining like a bloody beacon out there in the moonlight.'

'I'll be all right.'

'You will not,' he said. 'Take it off, Gordon, please. I'll see you in three minutes.' He disappeared into his caravan behind the filling-station, and I went indoors and changed my yellow pullover for a blue one.

When we met again outside, Claud was dressed in a pair of black trousers and a dark-green turtleneck sweater. On his head he wore a brown cloth cap with the peak pulled down low over his eyes, and he looked like an apache actor out of a nightclub.

'What's under there?' I asked, seeing the bulge at his waistline.

He pulled up his sweater and showed me two thin but very large white cotton sacks which were bound neat and tight around his belly. 'To carry the stuff,' he said darkly.

'I see.'

'Let's go,' he said.

'I still think we ought to take the car.'

'It's too risky. They'll see it parked.'

'But it's over three miles up to that wood.'

'Yes,' he said. 'And I suppose you realize we can get six months in the clink if they catch us.'

'You never told me that.'

'Didn't I?'

'I'm not coming,' I said. 'It's not worth it.'

'The walk will do you good, Gordon. Come on.'

It was a calm sunny evening with little wisps of brilliant white cloud hanging motionless in the sky, and the valley was cool and very quiet as the two of us began walking together along the grass verge on the side of the road that ran between the hills towards Oxford.

'You got the raisins?' Claud asked.

'They're in my pocket.'

'Good,' he said. 'Marvellous.'

Ten minutes later we turned left off the main road into a narrow lane with high hedges on either side and from now on it was all uphill.

'How many keepers are there?' I asked.

'Three.'

Claud threw away a half-finished cigarette. A minute later he lit another.

'I don't usually approve of new methods,' he said. 'Not on this sort of a job.'

'Of course.'

'But by God, Gordon, I think we're on to a hot one this time.'

'You do?'

'There's no question about it.'

'I hope you're right.'

'It'll be a milestone in the history of poaching,' he said.

'But don't you go telling a single soul how we've done it, you understand. Because if this ever leaked out we'd have every bloody fool in the district doing the same thing and there wouldn't be a pheasant left.'

'I won't say a word.'

'You ought to be very proud of yourself,' he went on. 'There's been men with brains studying this problem for hundreds of years and not one of them's ever come up with anything even a quarter as artful as you have. Why didn't you tell me about it before?'

'You never invited my opinion,' I said.

And that was the truth. In fact, up until the day before, Claud had never even offered to discuss with me the sacred subject of poaching. Often enough, on a summer's evening when work was finished, I had seen him with cap on head sliding quietly out of his caravan and disappearing up the road towards the woods; and sometimes, watching him through the windows of the filling-station, I would find myself wondering exactly what he was going to do, what wily tricks he was going to practise all alone up there under the trees in the dead of night. He seldom came back until very late, and never, absolutely never did he bring any of the spoils with him personally on his return. But the following afternoon – and I couldn't imagine how he did it – there would always be a pheasant or a hare or a brace of partridges hanging up in the shed behind the filling-station for us to eat.

This summer he had been particularly active, and during the last couple of months he had stepped up the tempo to a point where he was going out four and sometimes five nights a week. But that was not all. It seemed to me that recently his whole attitude towards poaching had undergone a subtle and mysterious change. He was more purposeful about it now, more tight-lipped and intense than before, and I had the impression that this was not so much a game any longer as a crusade, a sort of private war that Claud was waging single-handed against an invisible and hated enemy.

But who?

I wasn't sure about this, but I had a suspicion that it was none other than the famous Mr Victor Hazel himself, the owner of the land and the pheasants. Mr Hazel was a local brewer with an unbelievably arrogant manner. He was rich beyond words, and his property stretched for miles along either side of the valley. He was a self-made man with no charm at all and precious few virtues. He loathed all persons of humble station, having once been one of them himself, and he strove desperately to mingle with what he believed were the right kind of folk. He rode to hounds and gave shooting-parties and wore fancy waistcoats, and every weekday he drove an enormous black Rolls-Royce past the filling-station on his way to the brewery. As he flashed by, we would sometimes catch a glimpse of the great glistening brewer's face above the wheel, pink as a ham, all soft and inflamed from drinking too much beer.

Anyway, yesterday afternoon, right out of the blue, Claud had suddenly said to me, 'I'll be going on up to Hazel's woods again tonight. Why don't you come along?'

'Who, me?'

'It's about the last chance this year for pheasants,' he had said. 'The shooting-season opens Saturday and the birds'll be scattered all over the place after that – if there's any left.'

'Why the sudden invitation?' I had asked, greatly suspicious.

'No special reason, Gordon. No reason at all.'

'Is it risky?'

He hadn't answered this.

'I suppose you keep a gun or something hidden away up there?'

'A gun!' he cried, disgusted. 'Nobody ever *shoots* pheasants, didn't you know that? You've only got to fire a *cap-pistol* in Hazel's woods and the keepers'll be on you.'

'Then how do you do it?'

'Ah,' he said, and the eyelids drooped over the eyes, veiled and secretive.

There was a long pause. Then he said, 'Do you think you could keep your mouth shut if I was to tell you a thing or two?'

'Definitely.'

'I've never told this to anyone else in my whole life, Gordon.'

'I am greatly honoured,' I said. 'You can trust me completely.'

He turned his head, fixing me with pale eyes. The eyes were large and wet and ox-like, and they were so near to me that I could see my own face reflected upside down in the centre of each.

'I am now about to let you in on the three best ways in

the world of poaching a pheasant,' he said. 'And seeing that you're the guest on this little trip, I am going to give you the choice of which one you'd like us to use tonight. How's that?'

'There's a catch in this.'

'There's no catch, Gordon. I swear it.'

'All right, go on.'

'Now, here's the thing,' he said. 'Here's the first big secret.' He paused and took a long suck at his cigarette. 'Pheasants,' he whispered softly, 'is *crazy* about raisins.'

'Raisins?'

'Just ordinary raisins. It's like a mania with them. My dad discovered that more than forty years ago just like he discovered all three of these methods I'm about to describe to you now.'

'I thought you said your dad was a drunk.'

'Maybe he was. But he was also a great poacher, Gordon. Possibly the greatest there's ever been in the history of England. My dad studied poaching like a scientist.'

'Is that so?'

'I mean it. I really mean it.'

'I believe you.'

'Do you know,' he said, 'my dad used to keep a whole flock of prime cockerels in the back yard purely for experimental purposes.'

'Cockerels?'

'That's right. And whenever he thought up some new stunt for catching a pheasant, he'd try it out on a cockerel first to see how it worked. That's how he discovered about raisins. It's also how he invented the horsehair method.'

Claud paused and glanced over his shoulder as though to make sure that there was nobody listening. 'Here's how it's done,' he said. 'First you take a few raisins and you soak them overnight in water to make them nice and plump and juicy. Then you get a bit of good stiff horsehair and you cut it up into half-inch lengths. Then you push one of these lengths of horsehair through the middle of each raisin so that there's about an eighth of an inch of it sticking out on either side. You follow?'

'Yes.'

'Now – the old pheasant comes along and eats one of these raisins. Right? And you're watching him from behind a tree. So what then?'

'I imagine it sticks in his throat.'

'That's obvious, Gordon. But here's the amazing thing. Here's what my dad discovered. The moment this happens, the bird *never moves his feet again*! He becomes absolutely rooted to the spot, and there he stands pumping his silly neck up and down just like it was a piston, and all you've got to do is walk calmly out from the place where you're hiding and pick him up in your hands.'

'I don't believe that.'

'I swear it,' he said. 'Once a pheasant's had the horsehair you can fire a rifle in his ear and he won't even jump. It's just one of those unexplainable little things. But it takes a genius to discover it.'

He paused, and there was a gleam of pride in his eye now as he dwelt for a moment or two upon the memory of his father, the great inventor.

'So that's Method Number One,' he said. 'Method

Number Two is even more simple still. All you do is you have a fishing line. Then you bait the hook with a raisin and you fish for the pheasant just like you fish for a fish. You pay out the line about fifty yards and you lie there on your stomach in the bushes waiting till you get a bite. Then you haul him in.'

'I don't think your father invented that one.'

'It's very popular with fishermen,' he said, choosing not to hear me. 'Keen fishermen who can't get down to the seaside as often as they want. It gives them a bit of the old thrill. The only trouble is it's rather noisy. The pheasant squawks like hell as you haul him in, and then every keeper in the wood comes running.'

'What is Method Number Three?' I asked.

'Ah,' he said. 'Number Three's a real beauty. It was the last one my dad ever invented before he passed away.'

'His final great work?'

'Exactly, Gordon. And I can even remember the very day it happened, a Sunday morning it was, and suddenly my dad comes into the kitchen holding a huge white cockerel in his hands and he says, "I think I've got it!" There's a little smile on his face and a shine of glory in his eyes and he comes in very soft and quiet and he puts the bird down right in the middle of the kitchen table and he says, "By God I think I've got a good one this time!" "A good what?" Mum says, looking up from the sink. "Horace, take that filthy bird off my table." The cockerel has a funny little paper hat over its head, like an ice-cream cone upside down, and my dad is pointing to it proudly. "Stroke him," he says. "He won't move an inch." The cockerel starts scratching away at the paper hat with one of its feet, but the hat seems to be stuck on with glue and it won't come off. "No bird in the world is going to run away once you cover up his eyes," my dad says, and he starts poking the cockerel with his finger and pushing it around on the table, but it doesn't take the slightest bit of notice. "You can have this one," he says, talking to Mum. "You can kill it and dish it up for dinner as a celebration of what I have just invented." And then straight away he takes me by the arm and marches me quickly out the door and off we go over the fields and up into the big forest the other side of Haddenham which used to belong to the Duke of Buckingham, and in less than two hours we get five lovely fat pheasants with no more trouble than it takes to go out and buy them in a shop.'

Claud paused for breath. His eyes were huge and moist and dreamy as they gazed back into the wonderful world of his youth.

'I don't quite follow this,' I said. 'How did he get the paper hats over the pheasants' heads up in the woods?'

'You'd never guess it.'

'I'm sure I wouldn't.'

'Then here it is. First of all you dig a little hole in the ground. Then you twist a piece of paper into the shape of a cone and you fit this into the hole, hollow end upwards, like a cup. Then you smear the paper cup all around the inside with bird-lime and drop in a few raisins. At the same time you lay a trail of raisins along the ground leading up to it. Now – the old pheasant comes pecking along the trail, and when he gets to the hole he pops his head inside to gobble the raisins and the next thing he knows he's got a paper hat stuck over his eyes and he can't see a thing. Isn't it marvellous what some people think of, Gordon? Don't you agree?'

'Your dad was a genius,' I said.

'Then take your pick. Choose whichever one of the three methods you fancy and we'll use it tonight.'

'You don't think they're all just a trifle on the crude side, do you?'

'Crude!' he cried, aghast. 'Oh my God! And who's been having roasted pheasant in the house nearly every single day for the last six months and not a penny to pay?'

He turned and walked away towards the door of the workshop. I could see that he was deeply pained by my remark.

'Wait a minute,' I said. 'Don't go.'

'You want to come or don't you?'

'Yes, but let me ask you something first. I've just had a bit of an idea.'

'Keep it,' he said. 'You are talking about a subject you don't know the first thing about.'

'Do you remember that bottle of sleeping-pills the doc gave me last month when I had a bad back?'

'What about them?'

'Is there any reason why those wouldn't work on a pheasant?'

Claud closed his eyes and shook his head pityingly from side to side.

'Wait,' I said.

'It's not worth discussing,' he said. 'No pheasant in the

world is going to swallow those lousy red capsules. Don't you know any better than that?'

'You are forgetting the raisins,' I said. 'Now listen to this. We take a raisin. Then we soak it till it swells. Then we make a tiny slit in one side of it with a razor-blade. Then we hollow it out a little. Then we open up one of my red capsules and pour all the powder into the raisin. Then we get a needle and cotton and very carefully we sew up the slit. Now . . .'

Out of the corner of my eye, I saw Claud's mouth slowly beginning to open.

'Now,' I said. 'We have a nice clean-looking raisin with two and a half grains of seconal inside it, and let me tell *you* something now. That's enough dope to knock the average *man* unconscious, never mind about *birds*!'

I paused for ten seconds to allow the full impact of this to strike home.

'What's more, with this method we could operate on a really grand scale. We could prepare *twenty* raisins if we felt like it, and all we'd have to do is scatter them around the feeding-grounds at sunset and then walk away. Half an hour later we'd come back, and the pills would be beginning to work, and the pheasants would be up in the trees by then, roosting, and they'd be starting to feel groggy, and they'd be wobbling and trying to keep their balance, and soon every pheasant that had eaten *one single raisin* would keel over unconscious and fall to the ground. My dear boy, they'd be dropping out of the trees like apples, and all we'd have to do is walk around picking them up!'

Claud was staring at me, rapt.

'Oh Christ,' he said softly.

'And they'd never catch us either. We'd simply stroll through the woods dropping a few raisins here and there as we went, and even if they were *watching* us they wouldn't notice anything.'

'Gordon,' he said, laying a hand on my knee and gazing at me with eyes large and bright as two stars. 'If this thing works, it will *revolutionize* poaching.'

'I'm glad to hear it.'

'How many pills have you got left?' he asked.

'Forty-nine. There were fifty in the bottle and I've only used one.'

'Forty-nine's not enough. We want at least two hundred.'

'Are you mad!' I cried.

He walked slowly away and stood by the door with his back to me, gazing at the sky.

'Two hundred's the bare minimum,' he said quietly. 'There's really not much point in doing it unless we have two hundred.'

What is it now, I wondered. What the hell's he trying to do?

'This is the last chance we'll have before the season opens,' he said.

'I couldn't possibly get any more.'

'You wouldn't want us to come back empty-handed, would you?'

'But why so *many*?'

Claud turned his head and looked at me with large

innocent eyes. 'Why not?' he said gently. 'Do you have any objection?'

My God, I thought suddenly. The crazy bastard is out to wreck Mr Victor Hazel's opening-day shooting-party.

'You get us two hundred of those pills,' he said, 'and then it'll be worth doing.'

'I can't.'

'You could try, couldn't you?'

Mr Hazel's party took place on the first of October every year and it was a very famous event. Debilitated gentlemen in tweed suits, some with titles and some who were merely rich, motored in from miles around with their gun-bearers and dogs and wives, and all day long the noise of shooting rolled across the valley. There were always enough pheasants to go round, for each summer the woods were methodically restocked with dozens and dozens of young birds at incredible expense. I had heard it said that the cost of rearing and keeping each pheasant up to the time when it was ready to be shot was well over five pounds (which is approximately the price of two hundred loaves of bread). But to Mr Hazel it was worth every penny of it. He became, if only for a few hours, a big cheese in a little world and even the Lord Lieutenant of the County slapped him on the back and tried to remember his first name when he said good-bye.

'How would it be if we just reduced the dose?' Claud asked. 'Why couldn't we divide the contents of one capsule among four raisins?'

'I suppose you could if you wanted to.'

'But would a quarter of a capsule be strong enough for each bird?'

One simply had to admire the man's nerve. It was dangerous enough to poach a single pheasant up in those woods at this time of year and here he was planning to knock off the bloody lot.

'A quarter would be plenty,' I said.

'You're sure of that?'

'Work it out for yourself. It's all done by bodyweight. You'd still be giving about twenty times more than is necessary.'

'Then we'll quarter the dose,' he said, rubbing his hands. He paused and calculated for a moment. 'We'll have one hundred and ninety-six raisins!'

'Do you realize what that involves?' I said. 'They'll take hours to prepare.'

'What of it!' he cried. 'We'll go tomorrow instead. We'll soak the raisins overnight and then we'll have all morning and afternoon to get them ready.'

And that was precisely what we did.

Now, twenty-four hours later, we were on our way. We had been walking steadily for about forty minutes and we were nearing the point where the lane curved round to the right and ran along the crest of the hill towards the big wood where the pheasants lived. There was about a mile to go.

'I don't suppose by any chance these keepers might be carrying guns?' I asked.

'All keepers carry guns,' Claud said.

I had been afraid of that.

'It's for the vermin mostly.'

'Ah.'

'Of course there's no guarantee they won't take a pot at a poacher now and again.'

'You're joking.'

'Not at all. But they only do it from behind. Only when you're running away. They like to pepper you in the legs at about fifty yards.'

'They can't do that!' I cried. 'It's a criminal offence!'

'So is poaching,' Claud said.

We walked on awhile in silence. The sun was below the high hedge on our right now and the lane was in shadow.

'You can consider yourself lucky this isn't thirty years ago,' he went on. 'They used to shoot you on sight in those days.'

'Do you believe that?'

'I know it,' he said. 'Many's the night when I was a nipper I've gone into the kitchen and seen my old dad lying face downwards on the table and Mum standing over him digging the grapeshot out of his buttocks with a potato knife.'

'Stop,' I said. 'It makes me nervous.'

'You believe me, don't you?'

'Yes, I believe you.'

'Towards the end he was so covered in tiny little white scars he looked exactly like it was snowing.'

'Yes,' I said. 'All right.'

'Poacher's arse, they used to call it,' Claud said. 'And there wasn't a man in the whole village who didn't have a bit of it one way or another. But my dad was the champion.'

'Good luck to him,' I said.

'I wish to hell he was here now,' Claud said, wistful. 'He'd have given anything in the world to be coming with us on this job tonight.'

'He could take my place,' I said. 'Gladly.'

We had reached the crest of the hill and now we could see the wood ahead of us, huge and dark with the sun going down behind the trees and little sparks of gold shining through.

'You'd better let me have those raisins,' Claud said.

I gave him the bag and he slid it gently into his trouser pocket.

'No talking once we're inside,' he said. 'Just follow me and try not to go snapping any branches.'

Five minutes later we were there. The lane ran right up to the wood itself and then skirted the edge of it for about three hundred yards with only a little hedge between. Claud slipped through the hedge on all fours and I followed.

It was cool and dark inside the wood. No sunlight came in at all.

'This is spooky,' I said.

'Ssshh!'

Claud was very tense. He was walking just ahead of me, picking his feet up high and putting them down gently on the moist ground. He kept his head moving all the time, the eyes sweeping slowly from side to side, searching for danger. I tried doing the same, but soon I began to see a keeper behind every tree, so I gave it up.

Then a large patch of sky appeared ahead of us in the

roof of the forest and I knew that this must be the clearing. Claud had told me that the clearing was the place where the young birds were introduced into the woods in early July, where they were fed and watered and guarded by the keepers, and where many of them stayed from force of habit until the shooting began.

'There's always plenty of pheasants in the clearing,' he had said.

'Keepers too, I suppose.'

'Yes, but there's thick bushes all around and that helps.'

We were now advancing in a series of quick crouching spurts, running from tree to tree and stopping and waiting and listening and running on again, and then at last we were kneeling safely behind a big clump of alder right on the edge of the clearing and Claud was grinning and nudging me in the ribs and pointing through the branches at the pheasants.

The place was absolutely stiff with birds. There must have been two hundred of them at least strutting around among the tree-stumps.

'You see what I mean?' Claud whispered.

It was an astonishing sight, a sort of poacher's dream come true. And how close they were! Some of them were not more than ten paces from where we knelt. The hens were plump and creamy-brown and they were so fat their breast-feathers almost brushed the ground as they walked. The cocks were slim and beautiful, with long tails and brilliant red patches around the eyes, like scarlet spectacles. I glanced at Claud. His big ox-like face was transfixed in ecstasy. The mouth was slightly open and the eyes had a kind of glazy look about them as they stared at the pheasants.

I believe that all poachers react in roughly the same way as this on sighting game. They are like women who sight large emeralds in a jeweller's window, the only difference being that the women are less dignified in the methods they employ later on to acquire the loot. Poacher's arse is nothing to the punishment that a female is willing to endure.

'Ah-ha,' Claud said softly. 'You see the keeper?'

'Where?'

'Over the other side, by that big tree. Look carefully.'

'My God!'

'It's all right. He can't see *us*.'

We crouched close to the ground, watching the keeper. He was a smallish man with a cap on his head and a gun under his arm. He never moved. He was like a little post standing there.

'Let's go,' I whispered.

The keeper's face was shadowed by the peak of his cap, but it seemed to me that he was looking directly at us.

'I'm not staying here,' I said.

'Hush,' Claud said.

Slowly, never taking his eyes from the keeper, he reached into his pocket and brought out a single raisin. He placed it in the palm of his right hand, and then quickly, with a little flick of the wrist, he threw the raisin high into the air. I watched it as it went sailing over the bushes and I saw it land within a yard or so of two henbirds standing together beside an old tree-stump. Both birds turned their heads sharply at the drop of the raisin. Then one of them hopped over and made a quick peck at the ground and that must have been it.

I glanced up at the keeper. He hadn't moved.

Claud threw a second raisin into the clearing; then a third, and a fourth, and a fifth.

At this point, I saw the keeper turn away his head in order to survey the wood behind him.

Quick as a flash, Claud pulled the paper bag out of his pocket and tipped a huge pile of raisins into the cup of his right hand.

'Stop,' I said.

But with a great sweep of the arm he flung the whole handful high over the bushes into the clearing.

They fell with a soft little patter, like raindrops on dry leaves, and every single pheasant in the place must either have seen them coming or heard them fall. There was a flurry of wings and a rush to find the treasure.

The keeper's head flicked round as though there were a spring inside his neck. The birds were all pecking away madly at the raisins. The keeper took two quick paces forward and for a moment I thought he was going in to investigate. But then he stopped, and his face came up and his eyes began travelling slowly around the perimeter of the clearing.

'Follow me,' Claud whispered. 'And *keep down*.' He started crawling away swiftly on all fours, like some kind of a monkey.

I went after him. He had his nose close to the ground and his huge tight buttocks were winking at the sky and it was easy to see now how poacher's arse had come to be an occupational disease among the fraternity.

We went along like this for about a hundred yards.

'Now run,' Claud said.

We got to our feet and ran, and a few minutes later we emerged through the hedge into the lovely open safety of the lane.

'It went marvellous,' Claud said, breathing heavily. 'Didn't it go absolutely marvellous?' The big face was scarlet and glowing with triumph.

'It was a mess,' I said.

'What!' he cried.

'Of course it was. We can't possibly go back now. That keeper knows there was someone there.'

'He knows nothing,' Claud said. 'In another five minutes it'll be pitch dark inside the wood and he'll be sloping off home to his supper.'

'I think I'll join him.'

'You're a great poacher,' Claud said. He sat down on the grassy bank under the hedge and lit a cigarette.

The sun had set now and the sky was a pale smoke blue, faintly glazed with yellow. In the woods behind us the shadows and the spaces in between the trees were turning from grey to black.

'How long does a sleeping-pill take to work?' Claud asked.

'Look out,' I said. 'There's someone coming.'

The man had appeared suddenly and silently out of the dusk and he was only thirty yards away when I saw him.

'Another bloody keeper,' Claud said.

We both looked at the keeper as he came down the lane towards us. He had a shotgun under his arm and there was a black Labrador walking at his heels. He stopped when he was a few paces away and the dog stopped with him and stayed behind him, watching us through the keeper's legs.

'Good evening,' Claud said, nice and friendly.

This one was a tall bony man about forty with a swift eye and a hard cheek and hard dangerous hands.

'I know you,' he said softly, coming closer. 'I know the both of you.'

Claud didn't answer this.

'You're from the fillin'-station. Right?'

His lips were thin and dry, with some sort of a brownish crust over them.

'You're Cubbage and Hawes and you're from the fillin'-station on the main road. Right?'

'What are we playing?' Claud said. 'Twenty Questions?'

The keeper spat out a big gob of spit and I saw it go floating through the air and land with a plop on a patch of dry dust six inches from Claud's feet. It looked like a little baby oyster lying there.

'Beat it,' the man said. 'Go on. Get out.'

Claud sat on the bank smoking his cigarette and looking at the gob of spit.

'Go on,' the man said. 'Get out.'

When he spoke, the upper lip lifted above the gum and I could see a row of small discoloured teeth, one of them black, the others quince and ochre.

'This happens to be a public highway,' Claud said. 'Kindly do not molest us.'

The keeper shifted the gun from his left arm to his right.

'You're loiterin',' he said, 'with intent to commit a felony. I could run you in for that.'

'No you couldn't,' Claud said.

All this made me rather nervous.

'I've had my eye on you for some time,' the keeper said, looking at Claud.

'It's getting late,' I said. 'Shall we stroll on?'

Claud flipped away his cigarette and got slowly to his feet. 'All right,' he said. 'Let's go.'

We wandered off down the lane the way we had come, leaving the keeper standing there, and soon the man was out of sight in the half-darkness behind us.

'That's the head keeper,' Claud said. 'His name is Rabbetts.'

'Let's get the hell out,' I said.

'Come in here,' Claud said.

There was a gate on our left leading into a field and we climbed over it and sat down behind the hedge.

'Mr Rabbetts is also due for his supper,' Claud said. 'You mustn't worry about him.'

We sat quietly behind the hedge waiting for the keeper to walk past us on his way home. A few stars were showing and a bright three-quarter moon was coming up over the hills behind us in the east.

'Here he is,' Claud whispered. 'Don't move.'

The keeper came loping softly up the lane with the dog padding quick and soft-footed at his heels, and we watched them through the hedge as they went by.

'He won't be coming back tonight,' Claud said.

'How do you know that?'

'A keeper never waits for you in the wood if he knows where you live. He goes to your house and hides outside and watches for you to come back.'

'That's worse.'

'No, it isn't, not if you dump the loot somewhere else before you go home. He can't touch you then.'

'What about the other one, the one in the clearing?'

'He's gone too.'

'You can't be sure of that.'

'I've been studying these bastards for months, Gordon, honest I have. I know all their habits. There's no danger.'

Reluctantly I followed him back into the wood. It was pitch dark in there now and very silent, and as we moved cautiously forward the noise of our footsteps seemed to go echoing around the walls of the forest as though we were walking in a cathedral.

'Here's where we threw the raisins,' Claud said.

I peered through the bushes.

The clearing lay dim and milky in the moonlight.

'You're quite sure the keeper's gone?'

'I *know* he's gone.'

I could just see Claud's face under the peak of his cap, the pale lips, the soft pale cheeks, and the large eyes with a little spark of excitement dancing slowly in each.

'Are they roosting?'

'Yes.'

'Whereabouts?'

'All around. They don't go far.'

'What do we do next?'

'We stay here and wait. I brought you a light,' he added, and he handed me one of those small pocket flashlights shaped like a fountain-pen. 'You may need it.'

I was beginning to feel better. 'Shall we see if we can spot some of them sitting in the trees?' I said.

'No.'

'I should like to see how they look when they're roosting.'

'This isn't a nature-study,' Claud said. 'Please be quiet.'

We stood there for a long time waiting for something to happen.

'I've just had a nasty thought,' I said. 'If a bird can keep its balance on a branch when it's asleep, then surely there isn't any reason why the pills should make it fall down.'

Claud looked at me quick.

'After all,' I said, 'it's not dead. It's still only sleeping.'

'It's doped,' Claud said.

'But that's just a *deeper* sort of sleep. Why should we expect it to fall down just because it's in a *deeper* sleep?'

There was a gloomy silence.

'We should've tried it with chickens,' Claud said. 'My dad would've done that.'

'Your dad was a genius,' I said.

At that moment there came a soft thump from the wood behind us.

'Hey!'

'Ssshh!'

We stood listening.

Thump.

'There's another!'

It was a deep muffled sound as though a bag of sand had been dropped from about shoulder height.

Thump!

'They're pheasants!' I cried.

'Wait!'

'I'm sure they're pheasants!'

Thump! Thump!

'You're right!'

We ran back into the wood.

'Where were they?'

'Over here! Two of them were over here!'

'I thought they were this way.'

'Keep looking!' Claud shouted. 'They can't be far.'

We searched for about a minute.

'Here's one!' he called.

When I got to him he was holding a magnificent cock-bird in both hands. We examined it closely with our flashlights.

'It's doped to the gills,' Claud said. 'It's still alive, I can feel its heart, but it's doped to the bloody gills.'

Thump!

'There's another!'

Thump! Thump!

'Two more!'

Thump!

Thump! Thump! Thump!

'Jesus Christ!'

Thump! Thump! Thump! Thump!

Thump! Thump!

All around us the pheasants were starting to rain down out of the trees. We began rushing around madly in the dark, sweeping the ground with our flashlights.

Thump! Thump! Thump! This lot fell almost on top of me. I was right under the tree as they came down and I found all three of them immediately – two cocks and a hen. They were limp and warm, the feathers wonderfully soft in the hand.

'Where shall I put them?' I called out. I was holding them by the legs.

'Lay them here, Gordon! Just pile them up here where it's light!'

Claud was standing on the edge of the clearing with the moonlight streaming down all over him and a great bunch of pheasants in each hand. His face was bright, his eyes big and bright and wonderful, and he was staring around him like a child who has just discovered that the whole world is made of chocolate.

Thump!

Thump! Thump!

'I don't like it,' I said. 'It's too many.'

'It's beautiful!' he cried and he dumped the birds he was carrying and ran off to look for more.

Thump! Thump! Thump! Thump!

Thump!

It was easy to find them now. There were one or two lying under every tree. I quickly collected six more, three in each hand, and ran back and dumped them with the others. Then six more. Then six more after that.

And still they kept falling.

Claud was in a whirl of ecstasy now, dashing about like a mad ghost under the trees. I could see the beam of his flashlight waving around in the dark and each time he found a bird he gave a little yelp of triumph.

Thump! Thump! Thump!

'That bugger Hazel ought to hear this!' he called out.

'Don't shout,' I said. 'It frightens me.'

'What's that?'

'Don't *shout*. There might be keepers.'

'Screw the keepers!' he cried. 'They're all eating!'

For three or four minutes, the pheasants kept on falling. Then suddenly they stopped.

'Keep searching!' Claud shouted. 'There's plenty more on the ground!'

'Don't you think we ought to get out while the going's good?'

'No,' he said.

We went on searching. Between us we looked under every tree within a hundred yards of the clearing, north, south, east and west, and I think we found most of them in the end. At the collecting-point there was a pile of pheasants as big as a bonfire.

'It's a miracle,' Claud was saying. 'It's a bloody miracle.' He was staring at them in a kind of trance.

'We'd better just take half a dozen each and get out quick,' I said.

'I would like to count them, Gordon.'

'There's no time for that.'

'I must count them.'

'No,' I said. 'Come on.'

'One . . .

'Two . . .

'Three . . .

'Four . . .'

He began counting them very carefully, picking up each bird in turn and laying it carefully to one side. The moon was directly overhead now and the whole clearing was brilliantly illuminated.

'I'm not standing around here like this,' I said. I walked back a few paces and hid myself in the shadows, waiting for him to finish.

'A hundred and seventeen . . . a hundred and eighteen . . . a hundred and nineteen . . . *a hundred and twenty*!' he cried. '*One hundred and twenty birds!* It's an all-time record!'

I didn't doubt it for a moment.

'The most my dad ever got in one night was fifteen and he was drunk for a week afterwards!'

'You're the champion of the world,' I said. 'Are you ready now?'

'One minute,' he answered and he pulled up his sweater and proceeded to unwind the two big white cotton sacks from around his belly. 'Here's yours,' he said, handing one of them to me. 'Fill it up quick.'

The light of the moon was so strong I could read the small print along the base of the sack. J. W. CRUMP, it said. KESTON FLOUR MILLS, LONDON SW17.

'You don't think that bastard with the brown teeth is watching us this very moment from behind a tree?'

'There's no chance of that,' Claud said. 'He's down at

the filling-station like I told you, waiting for us to come home.'

We started loading the pheasants into the sacks. They were soft and floppy-necked and the skin underneath the feathers was still warm.

'There'll be a taxi waiting for us in the lane,' Claud said.

'What?'

'I always go back in a taxi, Gordon, didn't you know that?'

I told him I didn't.

'A taxi is anonymous,' Claud said. 'Nobody knows who's inside a taxi except the driver. My dad taught me that.'

'Which driver?'

'Charlie Kinch. He's only too glad to oblige.'

We finished loading the pheasants, and I tried to hump my bulging sack on to my shoulder. My sack had about sixty birds inside it, and it must have weighed a hundred-weight and a half, at least. 'I can't carry this,' I said. 'We'll have to leave some of them behind.'

'Drag it,' Claud said. 'Just pull it behind you.'

We started off through the pitch-black woods, pulling the pheasants behind us. 'We'll never make it all the way back to the village like this,' I said.

'Charlie's never let me down yet,' Claud said.

We came to the margin of the wood and peered through the hedge into the lane. Claud said, 'Charlie boy' very softly and the old man behind the wheel of the taxi not five yards away poked his head out into the moonlight and gave us a sly toothless grin. We slid through the hedge, dragging the sacks after us along the ground.

'Hullo!' Charlie said. 'What's this?'

'It's cabbages,' Claud told him. 'Open the door.'

Two minutes later we were safely inside the taxi, cruising slowly down the hill towards the village.

It was all over now bar the shouting. Claud was triumphant, bursting with pride and excitement, and he kept leaning forward and tapping Charlie Kinch on the shoulder and saying, 'How about it, Charlie? How about this for a haul?' and Charlie kept glancing back pop-eyed at the huge bulging sacks lying on the floor between us and saying, 'Jesus Christ, man, how did you do it?'

'There's six brace of them for you, Charlie,' Claud said. And Charlie said, 'I reckon pheasants is going to be a bit scarce up at Mr Victor Hazel's opening-day shoot this year,' and Claud said, 'I imagine they are, Charlie, I imagine they are.'

'What in God's name are you going to do with a hundred and twenty pheasants?' I asked.

'Put them in cold storage for the winter,' Claud said. 'Put them in with the dogmeat in the deep-freeze at the filling-station.'

'Not tonight, I trust?'

'No, Gordon, not tonight. We leave them at Bessie's house tonight.'

'Bessie who?'

'Bessie Organ.'

'Bessie *Organ*!'

'Bessie always delivers my game, didn't you know that?'

'I don't know anything,' I said. I was completely stunned. Mrs Organ was the wife of the Reverend Jack Organ, the local vicar.

'Always choose a respectable woman to deliver your game,' Claud announced. 'That's correct, Charlie, isn't it?'

'Bessie's a right smart girl,' Charlie said.

We were driving through the village now and the street-lamps were still on and the men were wandering home from the pubs. I saw Will Prattley letting himself in quietly by the side-door of his fishmonger's shop and Mrs Prattley's head was sticking out of the window just above him, but he didn't know it.

'The vicar is very partial to roasted pheasant,' Claud said.

'He hangs it eighteen days,' Charlie said, 'then he gives it a couple of good shakes and all the feathers drop off.'

The taxi turned left and swung in through the gates of the vicarage. There were no lights on in the house and nobody met us. Claud and I dumped the pheasants in the coal shed at the rear, and then we said good-bye to Charlie Kinch and walked back in the moonlight to the filling-station, empty-handed. Whether or not Mr Rabbetts was watching us as we went in, I do not know. We saw no sign of him.

'Here she comes,' Claud said to me the next morning.

'Who?'

'Bessie – Bessie Organ.' He spoke the name proudly and with a slight proprietary air, as though he were a general referring to his bravest officer.

I followed him outside.

'Down there,' he said, pointing.

Far away down the road I could see a small female figure advancing towards us.

'What's she pushing?' I asked.

Claud gave me a sly look.

'There's only one safe way of delivering game,' he announced, 'and that's under a baby.'

'Yes,' I murmured, 'yes, of course.'

'That'll be young Christopher Organ in there, aged one and a half. He's a lovely child, Gordon.'

I could just make out the small dot of a baby sitting high up in the pram, which had its hood folded down.

'There's sixty or seventy pheasants at least under that little nipper,' Claud said happily. 'You just imagine that.'

'You can't put sixty or seventy pheasants in a pram.'

'You can if it's got a deep well underneath it, and if you take out the mattress and pack them in tight, right up to the top. All you need then is a sheet. You'll be surprised how little room a pheasant takes up when it's limp.'

We stood beside the pumps waiting for Bessie Organ to arrive. It was one of those warm windless September mornings with a darkening sky and a smell of thunder in the air.

'Right through the village bold as brass,' Claud said. 'Good old Bessie.'

'She seems in rather a hurry to me.'

Claud lit a new cigarette from the stub of the old one. 'Bessie is never in a hurry,' he said.

'She certainly isn't walking normal,' I told him. 'You look.'

He squinted at her through the smoke of his cigarette.

Then he took the cigarette out of his mouth and looked again.

'Well?' I said.

'She does seem to be going a tiny bit quick, doesn't she?' he said carefully.

'She's going damn quick.'

There was a pause. Claud was beginning to stare very hard at the approaching woman.

'Perhaps she doesn't want to be caught in the rain, Gordon. I'll bet that's exactly what it is, she thinks it's going to rain and she don't want the baby to get wet.'

'Why doesn't she put the hood up?'

He didn't answer this.

'She's *running*!' I cried. 'Look!' Bessie had suddenly broken into a full sprint.

Claud stood very still, watching the woman; and in the silence that followed I fancied I could hear a baby screaming.

'What's up?'

He didn't answer.

'There's something wrong with that baby,' I said. 'Listen.'

At this point, Bessie was about two hundred yards away from us but closing fast.

'Can you hear him now?' I said.

'Yes.'

'He's yelling his head off.'

The small shrill voice in the distance was growing louder every second, frantic, piercing, non-stop, almost hysterical.

'He's having a fit,' Claud announced.

'I think he must be.'

'That's why she's running, Gordon. She wants to get him in here quick and put him under a cold tap.'

'I'm sure you're right,' I said. 'In fact I know you're right. Just listen to that noise.'

'If it isn't a fit, you can bet your life it's something like it.'

'I quite agree.'

Claud shifted his feet uneasily on the gravel of the driveway. 'There's a thousand and one different things keep happening every day to little babies like that,' he said.

'Of course.'

'I knew a baby once who caught his fingers in the spokes of the pram wheel. He lost the lot. It cut them clean off.'

'Yes.'

'Whatever it is,' Claud said, 'I wish to Christ she'd stop running.'

A long truck loaded with bricks came up behind Bessie and the driver slowed down and poked his head out the window to stare. Bessie ignored him and flew on, and she was so close now I could see her big red face with the mouth wide open, panting for breath. I noticed she was wearing white gloves on her hands, very prim and dainty, and there was a funny little white hat to match perched right on the top of her head, like a mushroom.

Suddenly, out of the pram, straight up into the air, flew an enormous pheasant!

Claud let out a cry of horror.

The fool in the truck going along beside Bessie started roaring with laughter.

The pheasant flapped around drunkenly for a few

seconds, then it lost height and landed in the grass by the side of the road.

A grocer's van came up behind the truck and began hooting to get by. Bessie kept running.

Then – *whoosh!* – a second pheasant flew up out of the pram.

Then a third, and a fourth. Then a fifth.

'My God!' I said. 'It's the pills! They're wearing off!'

Claud didn't say anything.

Bessie covered the last fifty yards at a tremendous pace, and she came swinging into the driveway of the filling-station with birds flying up out of the pram in all directions.

'What the hell's going on?' she cried.

'Go round the back!' I shouted. 'Go round the back!' But she pulled up sharp against the first pump in the line, and before we could reach her she had seized the screaming infant in her arms and dragged him clear.

'No! No!' Claud cried, racing towards her. 'Don't lift the baby! Put him back! Hold down the sheet!' But she wasn't even listening, and with the weight of the child suddenly lifted away, a great cloud of pheasants rose up out of the pram, fifty or sixty of them, at least, and the whole sky above us was filled with huge brown birds flapping their wings furiously to gain height.

Claud and I started running up and down the driveway waving our arms to frighten them off the premises. 'Go away!' we shouted. 'Shoo! Go away!' But they were too dopey still to take any notice of us and within half a minute down they came again and settled themselves like a swarm of locusts all over the front of my filling-station. The place was covered with them. They sat wing to wing along the edges of the roof and on the concrete canopy that came out over the pumps, and a dozen at least were clinging to the sill of the office window. Some had flown down on to the rack that held the bottles of lubricating-oil, and others were sliding about on the bonnets of my second-hand cars. One cockbird with a fine tail was perched superbly on top of a petrol pump, and quite a number, those that were too drunk to stay aloft, simply squatted in the driveway at our feet, fluffing their feathers and blinking their small eyes.

Across the road, a line of cars had already started forming behind the brick-lorry and the grocery-van, and people were opening their doors and getting out and beginning to cross over to have a closer look. I glanced at my watch. It was twenty to nine. Any moment now, I thought, a large black car is going to come streaking along the road from the direction of the village, and the car will be a Rolls, and the face behind the wheel will be the great glistening brewer's face of Mr Victor Hazel.

'They near pecked him to pieces!' Bessie was shouting, clasping the screaming baby to her bosom.

'You go on home, Bessie,' Claud said, white in the face.

'Lock up,' I said. 'Put out the sign. We've gone for the day.'

The Visitor

First published in *Playboy* (May 1965)

Not long ago, a large wooden case was deposited at the door of my house by the railway delivery service. It was an unusually strong and well-constructed object, and made of some kind of dark red hardwood, not unlike mahogany. I lifted it with great difficulty on to a table in the garden, and examined it carefully. The stencilling on one side said that it had been shipped from Haifa by the m/v *Waverley Star*, but I could find no sender's name or address. I tried to think of somebody living in Haifa or thereabouts who might be wanting to send me a magnificent present. I could think of no one. I walked slowly to the toolshed, still pondering the matter deeply, and returned with a hammer and screwdriver. Then I began gently to prise open the top of the case.

Behold, it was filled with books! Extraordinary books! One by one, I lifted them all out (not yet looking inside any of them) and stacked them in three tall piles on the table. There were twenty-eight volumes altogether, and very beautiful they were indeed. Each of them was identically and superbly bound in rich green morocco, with the initials O.H.C. and a Roman numeral (I to XXVIII) tooled in gold upon the spine.

I took up the nearest volume, number XVI, and opened it. The unlined white pages were filled with a neat small handwriting in black ink. On the title page was written '1934'. Nothing else. I took up another volume, number XXI. It contained more manuscript in the same handwriting, but on the title page it said '1939'. I put it down and pulled out Vol. I, hoping to find a preface of some kind there, or perhaps the author's name. Instead, I found an envelope inside the cover. The envelope was addressed to me. I took out the letter it contained and glanced quickly at the signature. 'Oswald Hendryks Cornelius', it said.

It was Uncle Oswald!

No member of the family had heard from Uncle Oswald for over thirty years. The letter was dated 10 March 1964, and until its arrival, we could only assume that he still existed. Nothing was really known about him except that he lived in France, that he travelled a great deal, that he was a wealthy bachelor with unsavoury but glamorous habits who steadfastly refused to have anything to do with his own relatives. The rest was all rumour and hearsay, but the rumours were so splendid and the hearsay so exotic that Oswald had long since become a shining hero and a legend to us all.

'My dear boy,' the letter began

I believe that you and your three sisters are my closest surviving blood relations. You are therefore my rightful heirs, and because I have made no will, all that I leave behind me when I die will be yours. Alas, I have nothing to leave. I used to have quite a lot, and the fact that I have recently disposed of it all in my own way is none of your business. As consolation, though, I am sending you my private diaries. These, I think, ought to remain in the family. They cover all the best years of my life, and it will do you no harm to read them. But if you show them around or lend them out to strangers, you do so at your own great peril. If you publish them, then that, I should imagine, would be the end of both you and your publisher simultaneously. For you must understand that thousands of the heroines whom I mention in the diaries are still only half dead, and if you were foolish enough to splash their lily-white reputations with scarlet print, they would have your head on a salver in two seconds flat, and probably roast it in the oven for good measure. So you'd better be careful. I only met you once. That was years ago, in 1921, when your family was living in that large ugly house in South Wales. I was your big uncle and you were a very small boy, about five years old. I don't suppose you remember the young Norwegian nursemaid you had then. A remarkably clean, well-built girl she was, and exquisitely shaped even in her uniform with its ridiculous starchy white shield concealing her lovely bosom. The afternoon I was there, she was taking you for a walk in the woods to pick bluebells, and I asked if I might come along. And when we got well into the middle of the woods, I told you I'd give you a bar of chocolate if you could find your own way home. And you did (see Vol. III). You were a sensible child. Farewell – Oswald Hendryks Cornelius.

The sudden arrival of the diaries caused much excitement in the family, and there was a rush to read them. We were not disappointed. It was astonishing stuff – hiliarious, witty, exciting, and often quite touching as well. The man's vitality was unbelievable. He was always on the move, from city to city, from country to country, from woman to woman, and in between the women, he would be searching for spiders in Kashmir or tracking down a blue porcelain vase in Nanking. But the women always came first. Wherever he went, he left an endless trail of females in his wake, females ruffled and ravished beyond words, but purring like cats.

Twenty-eight volumes with exactly three hundred pages to each volume take a deal of reading, and there are precious few writers who could hold an audience over a distance like that. But Oswald did it. The narrative never seemed to lose its flavour, the pace seldom slackened, and almost without exception, every single entry, whether it was long or short, and whatever the subject, became a marvellous little individual story that was complete in itself. And at the end of it all, when the last page of the last volume had been read, one was left with the rather breathless feeling that this might just possibly be one of the major autobiographical works of our time.

If it were regarded solely as a chronicle of a man's amorous adventures, then without a doubt there was nothing to touch it. Casanova's *Memoirs* read like a parish magazine in comparison, and the famous lover himself, beside Oswald, appears positively undersexed.

There was social dynamite on every page; Oswald was right about that. But he was surely wrong in thinking that the explosions would all come from the women. What about their husbands, the humiliated cock-sparrows, the cuckolds? The cuckold, when aroused, is a very fierce bird indeed, and there would be thousands upon thousands of them rising up out of the bushes if *The Cornelius Diaries*, unabridged, saw the light of day while they were still alive. Publication, therefore, was right out of the question.

A pity, this. Such a pity, in fact, that I thought something ought to be done about it. So I sat down and reread the diaries from beginning to end in the hope that I might discover at least one complete passage which could be printed and published without involving both the publisher and myself in serious litigation. To my joy, I found no less than six. I showed them to a lawyer. He said he thought they *might* be 'safe', but he wouldn't guarantee it. One of them – 'The Sinai Desert Episode' – seemed 'safer' than the other five, he added.

So I have decided to start with that one and to offer it for publication right away, at the end of this short preface. If it is accepted and all goes well, then perhaps I shall release one or two more.

The Sinai entry is from the last volume of all, Vol. XXVIII, and is dated 24 August 1946. In point of fact, it is the *very last entry* of the last volume of all, the last thing Oswald ever wrote, and we have no record of where he went or what he did after that date. One can only guess. You shall have the entry verbatim in a moment, but first of all, and so that you may more easily understand some of the things Oswald says and does in his story, let me try to tell you a little about the man himself. Out of the mass of confession and opinion contained in those twenty-eight volumes, there emerges a fairly clear picture of his character.

At the time of the Sinai episode, Oswald Hendryks Cornelius was fifty-one years old, and he had, of course, never been married. 'I am afraid,' he was in the habit of saying, 'that I have been blessed, or should I call it burdened, with an uncommonly fastidious nature.'

In some ways, this was true, but in others, and especially in so far as marriage was concerned, the statement was the exact opposite of the truth.

The real reason Oswald had refused to get married was simply that he had never in his life been able to confine his attentions to one particular woman for longer than the time it took to conquer her. When that was done, he lost interest and looked around for another victim.

A normal man would hardly consider this a valid reason for remaining single, but Oswald was not a normal man. He was not even a normally polygamous man. He was, to be honest, such a wanton and incorrigible philanderer that no bride on earth would have put up with him for more than a few days, let alone for the duration of a honeymoon – although heaven knows there were enough who would have been willing to give it a try.

He was a tall, narrow person with a fragile and faintly aesthetic air. His voice was soft, his manner was courteous, and at first sight he seemed more like a gentleman-in-waiting to the Queen than a celebrated rapscallion. He never discussed his amorous affairs with other men, and a stranger, though he might sit and talk with him all evening, would be unable to observe the slightest sign of deceit in Oswald's clear blue eyes. He was, in fact, precisely the sort of man that an anxious father would be likely to choose to escort his daughter safely home.

But sit Oswald beside a *woman*, a woman who interested him, and instantaneously his eyes would change, and as he looked at her, a small dangerous spark would begin dancing slowly in the very centre of each pupil; and then he would set about her with his conversation, talking to her rapidly and cleverly and almost certainly more wittily than anyone else had ever done before. This was a gift he had, a most singular talent, and when he put his mind to it, he could make his words coil themselves round and round the listener until they held her in some sort of a mild hypnotic spell.

But it wasn't only his fine talk and the look in his eyes that fascinated the women. It was also his nose. (In Vol. XIV, Oswald includes, with obvious relish, a note written to him by a certain lady in which she describes such things as this in great detail.) It appears that when Oswald was aroused, something odd would begin to happen around the edges of his nostrils, a tightening of the rims, a visible flaring which enlarged the nostril holes and revealed whole areas of the bright red skin inside. This created a queer, wild, animalistic impression, and although it may not sound particularly attractive when described on paper, its effect upon the ladies was electric.

Almost without exception, women were drawn towards Oswald. In the first place, he was a man who refused to be owned at any price, and this automatically made him desirable. Add to this the unusual combination of a first-rate intellect, an abundance of charm and a reputation for excessive promiscuity, and you have a potent recipe.

Then again, and forgetting for a moment the disreputable and licentious angle, it should be noted that there were a number of other surprising facets to Oswald's character that in themselves made him a rather intriguing person. There was, for example, very little that he did not know about nineteenth-century Italian opera, and he had written a curious little manual upon the three composers Donizetti, Verdi and Ponchielli. In it, he listed by name all the important mistresses that these men had had during their lives, and he went on to examine, in a most serious vein, the relationship between creative passion and carnal passion, and the influence of the one upon the other, particularly as it affected the works of these composers.

Chinese porcelain was another of Oswald's interests, and he was acknowledged as something of an international authority in this field. The blue vases of the Tchin-Hoa period were his special love, and he had a small but exquisite collection of these pieces.

He also collected spiders and walking-sticks.

His collection of spiders, or more accurately, his collection of Arachnida, because it included scorpions and pedipalps, was possibly as comprehensive as any outside a museum, and his knowledge of the hundreds of genera and species was impressive. He maintained, incidentally (and probably correctly), that spiders' silk was superior in quality to the ordinary stuff spun by silkworms, and he never wore a tie that was made of any other material. He possessed about forty of these ties altogether, and in order to acquire them in the first place, and in order also to be able to add two new ties a year to his wardrobe, he had to keep thousands and thousands of *Arana* and *Epeira diademata* (the common English garden spiders) in an old conservatory in the garden of his country house outside Paris, where they bred and multiplied at approximately the same rate as they ate one another. From them, he collected the raw thread himself – no one else would enter that ghastly glasshouse – and sent it to Avignon, where it was reeled and thrown and scoured and dyed and made into cloth. From Avignon, the cloth was delivered directly to Sulka, who were enchanted by the whole business, and only too glad to fashion ties out of such a rare and wonderful material.

'But you can't *really* like spiders?' the women visitors would say to Oswald as he displayed his collection.

'Oh, but I adore them,' he would answer. 'Especially the females. They remind me so much of certain human females that I know. They remind me of my very favourite human females.'

'What nonsense, darling.'

'Nonsense? I think not.'

'It's rather insulting.'

'On the contrary, my dear, it is the greatest compliment I could pay. Did you not know, for instance, that the female spider is so savage in her love-making that the male is very lucky indeed if he escapes with his life at the end of it all. Only if he is exceedingly agile and marvellously ingenious will he get away in one piece.'

'Now, *Oswald*!'

'And the crab spider, my beloved, the teeny-weeny little crab spider is so dangerously passionate that her lover has to tie her down with intricate loops and knots of his own thread before he dares to embrace her . . .'

'Oh, *stop* it, Oswald, this *minute*!' the women would cry, their eyes shining.

Oswald's collection of walking-sticks was something else again. Every one of them had belonged either to a distinguished or a disgusting person, and he kept them all in his Paris apartment, where they were displayed in two long racks standing against the walls of the passage (or should one call it the highway?) which led from the living-room to the bedroom. Each stick had its own little ivory label above it, saying Sibelius, Milton, King Farouk, Dickens, Robespierre, Puccini, Oscar Wilde, Franklin Roosevelt, Goebbels, Queen Victoria, Toulouse-Lautrec, Hindenburg, Tolstoy, Laval, Sarah Bernhardt, Goethe, Voroshiloff, Cézanne, Tojo . . . There must have been over a hundred of them in all, some very beautiful, some very plain, some with gold or silver tops, and some with curly handles.

'Take down the Tolstoy,' Oswald would say to a pretty visitor. 'Go on, take it down . . . that's right . . . and now . . . now rub your own palm gently over the knob that has been worn to a shine by the great man himself. Is it not rather wonderful, the mere contact of your skin with that spot?'

'It is, rather, isn't it.'

'And now take the Goebbels and do the same thing. Do it properly, though. Allow your palm to fold tightly over the handle . . . good . . . and now . . . now lean your weight on it, lean hard, exactly as the little deformed doctor used to do . . . there . . . that's it . . . now stay like that for a minute or so and then tell me if you do not feel a thin finger of ice creeping all the way up your arm and into your chest.'

'It's terrifying!'

'Of course it is. Some people pass out completely. They keel right over.'

Nobody ever found it dull to be in Oswald's company, and perhaps that, more than anything else, was the reason for his success.

We come now to the Sinai episode. Oswald, during that month, had been amusing himself by motoring at a fairly leisurely pace down from Khartoum to Cairo. His car was a superlative prewar Lagonda which had been carefully stored in Switzerland during the war years, and as you can imagine, it was fitted with every kind of gadget under the sun. On the day before Sinai (23 August 1946), he was in Cairo, staying at Shepheard's Hotel, and that evening, after a series of impudent manoeuvres, he had succeeded in getting hold of a Moorish lady of supposedly aristocratic descent, called Isabella. Isabella happened to be the jealously guarded mistress of none other than a certain notorious and dyspeptic Royal Personage (there was still a monarchy in Egypt then). This was a typically Oswaldian move.

But there was more to come. At midnight, he drove the lady out to Giza and persuaded her to climb with him in the moonlight right to the very top of the great pyramid of Cheops.

'. . . There can be no safer place,' he wrote in the diary,

> nor a more romantic one, than the apex of a pyramid on a warm night when the moon is full. The passions are stirred not only by the magnificent view but also by that curious sensation of power that surges within the body whenever one surveys the world from a great height. And as for safety – this pyramid is exactly 481 feet high, which is 115 feet higher than the dome of St Paul's Cathedral, and from the summit one can observe all the approaches with the greatest of ease. No other boudoir on earth can offer this facility. None has so many emergency exits, either, so that if some sinister figure should happen to come clambering up in pursuit on one side of the pyramid, one has only to slip calmly and quietly down the other . . .

As it happened, Oswald had a very narrow squeak indeed that night. Somehow, the palace must have got word of the little affair, for Oswald, from his lofty moonlit pinnacle, suddenly observed *three* sinister figures, not one, closing in on three different sides, and starting to climb. But luckily for him, there is a fourth side to the great pyramid of Cheops, and by the time those Arab thugs had reached the top, the two lovers were already at the bottom and getting into the car.

The entry for 24 August takes up the story at exactly this point. It is reproduced here word for word and comma for comma as Oswald wrote it. Nothing has been altered or added or taken away:

24 August 1946

'He'll chop off Isabella's head if he catch her now,' Isabella said.

'Rubbish,' I answered, but I reckoned she was probably right.

'He'll chop off Oswald's head, too,' she said.

'Not mine, dear lady. I shall be a long way away from here when daylight comes. I'm heading straight up the Nile for Luxor immediately.'

We were driving quickly away from the pyramids now. It was about two thirty a.m.

'To Luxor?' she said.

'Yes.'

'And Isabella is going with you.'

'No,' I said.

'Yes,' she said.

'It is against my principles to travel with a lady,' I said.

I could see some lights ahead of us. They came from the Mena House Hotel, a place where tourists stay out in the desert, not far from the pyramids. I drove fairly close to the hotel and stopped the car.

'I'm going to drop you here,' I said. 'We had a fine time.'

'So you won't take Isabella to Luxor?'

'I'm afraid not,' I said. 'Come on, hop it.'

She started to get out of the car, then she paused with one foot on the road, and suddenly she swung round and poured out upon me a torrent of language so filthy yet so fluent that I had heard nothing like it from the lips of a lady since . . . well, since 1931, in Marrakesh, when the greedy old Duchess of Glasgow put her hand into a chocolate box and got nipped by a scorpion I happened to have placed there for safe-keeping (Vol. XIII, 5 June 1931).

'You are disgusting,' I said.

Isabella leaped out and slammed the door so hard the whole car jumped on its wheels. I drove off very fast. Thank heaven I was rid of her. I cannot abide bad manners in a pretty girl.

As I drove, I kept one eye on the mirror, but as yet no car seemed to be following me. When I came to the outskirts of Cairo, I began threading my way through the side roads, avoiding the centre of the city. I was not particularly worried. The royal watch-dogs were unlikely to carry the matter much further. All the same, it would have been foolhardy to go back to Shepheard's at this point. It wasn't necessary anyway, because all my baggage, except for a small valise, was with me in the car. I never leave suitcases behind me in my room when I go out of an evening in a foreign city. I like to be mobile.

I had no intention, of course, of going to Luxor. I wanted now to get away from Egypt altogether. I didn't like the country at all. Come to think of it, I never had. The place made me feel uncomfortable in my skin. It was the dirtiness of it all, I think, and the putrid smells. But then let us face it, it really is a rather squalid country; and I have a powerful suspicion, though I hate to say it, that the Egyptians wash themselves less thoroughly than any other peoples in the world – with the possible exception of the Mongolians. Certainly they do not wash their crockery to my taste. There was, believe it or not, a long, crusted, coffee-coloured lipmark stamped upon the rim of the cup they placed before me at breakfast yesterday. Ugh! It was repulsive! I kept staring at it and wondering whose slobbery lower lip had done the deed.

I was driving now through the narrow dirty streets of the eastern suburbs of Cairo. I knew precisely where I was going. I had made up my mind about that before I was even halfway down the pyramid with Isabella. I was going to Jerusalem. It was no distance to speak of, and it was a city that I always enjoyed. Furthermore, it was the quickest way out of Egypt. I would proceed as follows:

1. Cairo to Ismailia. About three hours driving. Sing an opera on the way, as usual. Arrive Ismailia 6–7 a.m. Take a room and have a two-hour sleep. Then shower, shave and breakfast.

2. At 10 a.m., cross over the Suez Canal by the Ismailia bridge and take the desert road across Sinai to the Palestine border. Make a search for scorpions en route in the Sinai Desert. Time, about four hours, arriving Palestine border 2 p.m.

3. From there, continue straight on to Jerusalem via Beersheba, reaching the King David Hotel in time for cocktails and dinner.

It was several years since I had travelled that particular road, but I remembered that the Sinai Desert was an outstanding place for scorpions. I badly wanted another female opisthophthalmus, a large one. My present specimen had the fifth segment of its tail missing, and I was ashamed of it.

It didn't take me long to find the main road to Ismailia, and as soon as I was on it, I settled the Lagonda down to a steady sixty-five miles an hour. The road was narrow, but it had a smooth surface, and there was no traffic. The Delta country lay bleak and dismal around me in the moonlight, the flat treeless fields, the ditches running between, and the black soil everywhere. It was inexpressibly dreary.

But it didn't worry *me*. I was no part of it. I was completely isolated in my own luxurious little shell, as snug as a hermit crab and travelling a lot faster. Oh, how I do love to be on the move, winging away to new people and new places and leaving the old ones far behind! Nothing in the world exhilarates me more than that. And how I despise the average citizen, who settles himself down upon one tiny spot of land with one asinine woman, to breed and stew and rot in that condition unto his life's end. And always with the same woman! I simply cannot *believe* that any man in his senses would put up with just one female day after day and year after year. Some of them, of course, don't. But millions pretend they do.

I myself have never, absolutely never permitted an intimate relationship to last for more than twelve hours. That is the furthest limit. Even eight hours is stretching it a bit, to my mind. Look what happened, for example, with Isabella. While we were upon the summit of the pyramid, she was a lady of scintillating parts, as pliant and playful as a puppy, and had I left her there to the mercy of those three Arab thugs, and skipped down on my own, all would have been well. But I foolishly stuck by her and helped her to descend, and as a result, the lovely lady turned into a vulgar screeching trollop, disgusting to behold.

What a world we live in! One gets no thanks these days for being chivalrous.

The Lagonda moved on smoothly through the night. Now for an opera. Which one should it be this time? I was in the mood for a Verdi. What about *Aida*? Of course! It must be *Aida* – the Egyptian opera! Most appropriate.

I began to sing. I was in exceptionally good voice tonight. I let myself go. It was delightful; and as I drove through the small town of Bilbeis, I was Aida herself, singing '*Numei pietà*', the beautiful concluding passage of the first scene.

Half an hour later, at Zagazig, I was Amonasro begging the King of Egypt to save the Ethiopian captives with '*Ma tu, re, tu signore possente*'.

Passing through El Abbasa, I was Rhadames, rendering '*Fuggiam gli adori nospiti*', and now I opened all the windows of the car so that this incomparable love song might reach the ears of the fellaheen snoring in their hovels along the roadside, and perhaps mingle with their dreams.

As I pulled into Ismailia, it was six o'clock in the morning and the sun was already climbing high in a milky-blue heaven, but I myself was in the terrible sealed-up dungeon with Aida, singing, '*O terra, addio; addio valle di pianti!*'

How swiftly the journey had gone. I drove to an hotel. The staff was just beginning to stir. I stirred them up some more and got the best room available. The sheets and blanket on the bed looked as though they had been slept in by twenty-five unwashed Egyptians on twenty-five consecutive nights, and I tore them off with my own hands (which I scrubbed immediately afterward with antiseptic soap) and replaced them with my personal bedding. Then I set my alarm and slept soundly for two hours.

For breakfast I ordered a poached egg on a piece of toast. When the dish arrived – and I tell you, it makes my stomach curdle just to write about it – there was a *gleaming, curly, jet-black hair*, three inches long, lying diagonally across the yolk of my poached egg. It was too much. I leaped up from the table and rushed out of the dining-room. '*Addio!*' I cried, flinging some money at the cashier as I went by, '*Addio valle di pianti!*' And with that I shook the filthy dust of the hotel from my feet.

Now for the Sinai Desert. What a welcome change that would be. A real desert is one of the least contaminated places on earth, and Sinai was no exception. The road across it was a narrow strip of black tarmac about a hundred and forty miles long, with only a single filling-station and a group of huts at the halfway mark, at a place called B'ir Rawd Salim. Otherwise there was nothing but pure uninhabited desert all the way. It would be very hot at this time of year, and it was essential to carry drinking water in case of a breakdown. I therefore pulled up outside a kind of general store in the main street of Ismailia to get my emergency canister refilled.

I went in and spoke to the proprietor. The man had a nasty case of trachoma. The granulation on the under surfaces of his eyelids was so acute that the lids themselves were raised right up off the eyeballs – a beastly sight. I asked him if he would sell me a gallon of *boiled* water. He thought I was mad, and madder still when I insisted on following him back into his grimy kitchen to make sure that he did things properly. He filled a kettle with tap-water and placed it on a paraffin stove. The stove had a tiny little smoky yellow flame. The proprietor seemed very proud of the stove and of its performance. He stood admiring it, his head on one side. Then he suggested that I might prefer to go back and wait in the shop. He would bring me the water, he said, when it was ready. I refused to leave. I stood there watching the kettle like a lion, waiting for the water to boil; and while I was doing this, the breakfast scene suddenly started coming back to me in all its horror – the egg, the yolk and the hair. Whose hair was it that had lain embedded in the slimy yolk of my egg at breakfast? Undoubtedly it was the cook's hair. And when, pray, had the cook last washed his head? He had probably never washed his head. Very well, then. He was almost certainly verminous. But that in itself would not cause a hair to fall out. What *did* cause the cook's hair, then, to fall out on to my poached egg this morning as he transferred the egg from the pan to the plate? There is a reason for all things, and in this case the reason was obvious. The cook's scalp was infested with purulent seborrhoeic impetigo. And the hair itself, the long black hair that I might so easily have swallowed had I been less alert, was therefore swarming with millions and millions of living pathogenic cocci whose exact scientific name I have, happily, forgotten.

Can I, you ask, be absolutely sure that the cook had purulent seborrhoeic impetigo? Not absolutely sure – no. But if he hadn't, then he certainly had ringworm instead.

And what did that mean? I knew only too well what it meant. It meant that ten million microsporons had been clinging and clustering round that awful hair, waiting to go into my mouth.

I began to feel sick.

'The water boils,' the shopkeeper said triumphantly.

'Let it boil,' I told him. 'Give it eight minutes more. What is it you want me to get – typhus?'

Personally, I never drink plain water by itself if I can help it, however pure it may be. Plain water has no flavour at all. I take it, of course, as tea or as coffee, but even then I try to arrange for bottled Vichy or Malvern to be used in the preparation. I avoid tap-water. Tap-water is diabolical stuff. Often it is nothing more nor less than reclaimed sewage.

'Soon this water will be boiled away in steam,' the proprietor said, grinning at me with green teeth.

I lifted the kettle myself and poured the contents into my canister.

Back in the shop, I bought six oranges, a small water-melon and a slab of well-wrapped English chocolate. Then I returned to the Lagonda. Now at last I was away.

A few minutes later, I had crossed the sliding bridge that went over the Suez Canal just above Lake Timsah, and ahead of me lay the flat blazing desert and the little tarmac road stretching out before me like a black ribbon all the way to the horizon. I settled the Lagonda down to the usual steady sixty-five miles an hour, and I opened the windows wide. The air that came in was like the breath of an oven. The time was almost noon, and the sun was throwing its heat directly on to the roof of the car. My thermometer inside registered 103°. But as you know, a touch of warmth never bothers me so long as I am sitting still and am wearing suitable clothes – in this case a pair of cream-coloured linen slacks, a white Aertex shirt and a spider's-silk tie of the loveliest rich moss-green. I felt perfectly comfortable and at peace with the world.

For a minute or two I played with the idea of performing another opera en route – I was in the mood for *La Gioconda* – but after singing a few bars of the opening chorus, I began to perspire slightly; so I rang down the curtain, and lit a cigarette instead.

I was now driving through some of the finest scorpion country in the world, and I was eager to stop and make a search before I reached the halfway filling-station at B'ir Rawd Salim. I had so far met not a single vehicle nor seen a living creature since leaving Ismailia an hour before. This pleased me. Sinai was authentic desert. I pulled up on the side of the road and switched off the engine. I was thirsty, so I ate an orange. Then I put my white topee on my head, and eased myself slowly out of the car, out of my comfortable hermit-crab shell and into the sunlight. For a full minute I stood motionless in the middle of the road, blinking at the brilliance of the surroundings.

There was a blazing sun, a vast hot sky and beneath it all on every side a great pale sea of yellow sand that was not quite of this world. There were mountains now in the distance on the south side of the road, bare, pale, tanagra-coloured mountains faintly glazed with blue and purple, that rose up suddenly out of the desert and faded away in a haze of heat against the sky. The stillness was overpowering. There was no sound at all, no voice of bird or insect anywhere, and it gave me a queer godlike feeling to be standing there alone in the middle of such a splendid, hot, inhuman landscape – as though I were on another planet altogether, on Jupiter or Mars, or in some place more distant and desolate still, where never would the grass grow nor the clouds turn red.

I went to the boot of the car and took out my killing-box, my net and my trowel. Then I stepped off the road into the soft burning sand. I walked slowly for about a hundred yards into the desert, my eyes searching the ground. I was not looking for scorpions but the lairs of scorpions. The scorpion is a cryptozoic and nocturnal creature that hides all through the day either under a stone or in a burrow, according to its type. Only after the sun has gone down does it come out to hunt for food.

The one I wanted, opisthophthalmus, was a burrower, so I wasted no time turning over stones. I searched only for burrows. After ten or fifteen minutes, I had found none; but already the heat was getting to be too much for me, and I decided reluctantly to return to the car. I walked back very slowly, still watching the ground, and I had reached the road and was in the act of stepping on to it when all at once, in the sand, not more than twelve inches from the edge of the tarmac, I caught sight of a scorpion's burrow.

I put the killing-box and the net on the ground beside me. Then, with my little trowel, I began very cautiously to scrape away the sand all round the hole. This was an operation that never failed to excite me. It was like a treasure hunt – a treasure hunt with just the right amount of danger accompanying it to stir the blood. I could feel my heart beating away in my chest as I probed deeper and deeper into the sand.

And suddenly . . . there she was!

Oh, my heavens, what a whopper! A gigantic female scorpion, not opisthophthalmus, as I saw immediately, but pandinus, the other large African burrower. And clinging to her back – this was too good to be true! – swarming all over her, were one, two, three, four, five . . . a total of fourteen tiny babies! The mother was six inches long at least! Her children were the size of small revolver bullets. She had seen me now, the first human she had ever seen in her life, and her pincers were wide open, her tail was curled high over her back like a question mark, ready to strike. I took up the net, and slid it swiftly underneath her, and scooped her up. She twisted and squirmed, striking wildly in all directions with the end of her tail. I saw a single drop of venom fall through the mesh on to the sand. Quickly, I transferred her, together with all the offspring, to the killing-box, and closed the lid. Then I fetched the ether from the car, and poured it through the little gauze hole in the top of the box until the pad inside was well soaked.

How splendid she would look in my collection! The babies would, of course, fall away from her as they died, but I would stick them on again with glue in more or less their correct positions; and then I would be the proud possessor of a huge female pandinus with her own fourteen offspring on her back! I was extremely pleased.

I lifted the killing-box (I could feel her thrashing about furiously inside) and placed it in the boot, together with the net and trowel. Then I returned to my seat in the car, lit a cigarette, and drove on.

The more contented I am, the slower I drive. I drove quite slowly now, and it must have taken me nearly an hour more to reach B'ir Rawd Salim, the halfway station. It was a most unenticing place. On the left, there was a single gasoline pump and a wooden shack. On the right, there were three more shacks, each about the size of a potting-shed. The rest was desert. There was not a soul in sight. The time was twenty minutes before two in the afternoon, and the temperature inside the car was 106°.

What with the nonsense of getting the water boiled before leaving Ismailia, I had forgotten completely to fill up with gasoline before leaving, and my gauge was now registering slightly less than two gallons. I'd cut it rather fine – but no matter. I pulled in alongside the pump, and waited. Nobody appeared. I pressed the horn button, and the four tuned horns on the Lagonda shouted their wonderful '*Son gia mille e tre!*' across the desert. Nobody appeared. I pressed again.

sang the horns. Mozart's phrase sounded magnificent in these surroundings. But still nobody appeared. The inhabitants of B'ir Rawd Salim didn't give a damn, it seemed, about my friend Don Giovanni and the one thousand and three women he had deflowered in Spain.

At last, after I had played the horns no less than six times, the door of the hut behind the gasoline pump opened and a tallish man emerged and stood on the threshold, doing up his buttons with both hands. He took his time over this, and not until he had finished did he glance up at the Lagonda. I looked back at him through my open window. I saw him take the first step in my direction . . . he took it very, very slowly . . . Then he took a second step . . .

My God! I thought at once. The spirochetes have got him!

He had the slow, wobbly walk, the loose-limbed, high-stepping gait of a man with locomotor ataxia. With each step he took, the front foot was raised high in the air before him and brought down violently to the ground, as though he were stamping on a dangerous insect.

I thought: I had better get out of here. I had better start the motor and get the hell out of here before he reaches me. But I knew I couldn't. I *had* to have the gasoline. I sat in the car staring at the awful creature as he came stamping laboriously over the sand. He must have had the revolting disease for years and years, otherwise it wouldn't have developed into ataxia. *Tabes dorsalis*, they call it in professional circles, and pathologically this means that the victim is suffering from degeneration of the posterior columns of the spinal cord. But ah my foes and oh my friends, it is really a lot worse than that; it is a slow and merciless consuming of the actual nerve fibres of the body by syphilitic toxins.

The man – the Arab, I shall call him – came right up to the door of my side of the car and peered in through the open window. I leaned away from him, praying that he would come not an inch closer. Without a doubt, he was one of the most blighted humans I had ever seen. His face had the eroded, eaten-away look of an old wood-carving when the worm has been at it, and the sight of it made me wonder how many other diseases the man was suffering from, besides syphilis.

'Salaam,' he mumbled.

'Fill up the tank,' I told him.

He didn't move. He was inspecting the interior of the Lagonda with great interest. A terrible feculent odour came wafting in from his direction.

'Come along!' I said sharply. 'I want some gasoline!'

He looked at me and grinned. It was more of a leer than a grin, an insolent mocking leer that seemed to be saying, 'I am the king of the gasoline pump at B'ir Rawd Salim! Touch me if you dare!' A fly had settled in the corner of one of his eyes. He made no attempt to brush it away.

'You want gasoline?' he said, taunting me.

I was about to swear at him, but I checked myself just in time, and answered politely, 'Yes please, I would be very grateful.'

He watched me slyly for a few moments to be sure I wasn't mocking him, then he nodded as though satisfied now with my behaviour. He turned away and started slowly towards the rear of the car. I reached into the door-pocket for my bottle of Glenmorangie. I poured myself a stiff one, and sat sipping it. The man's face had been within a yard of my own; his foetid breath had come pouring into the car . . . and who knows how many billions of air-borne viruses might not have come pouring in with it? On such an occasion it is a fine thing to sterilize the mouth and throat with a drop of Highland whisky. The whisky is also a solace. I emptied the glass, and poured myself another. Soon I began to feel less alarmed. I noticed the watermelon lying on the seat beside me. I decided that a slice of it at this moment would be refreshing. I took my knife from its case and cut out a thick section. Then, with the point of the knife, I carefully picked out all the black seeds, using the rest of the melon as a receptacle.

I sat drinking the whisky and eating the melon. Both were delicious.

'Gasoline is done,' the dreadful Arab said, appearing at the window. 'I check water now, and oil.'

I would have preferred him to keep his hands off the Lagonda altogether, but rather than risk an argument, I said nothing. He went clumping off towards the front of the car, and his walk reminded me of a drunken Hitler Stormtrooper doing the goosestep in very slow motion.

Tabes dorsalis, as I live and breathe.

The only other disease to induce that queer high-stepping gait is chronic beriberi. Well – he probably had that one, too. I cut myself another slice of watermelon, and concentrated for a minute or so on taking out the seeds with the knife. When I looked up again, I saw that the Arab had raised the bonnet of the car on the right-hand side, and was bending over the engine. His head and shoulders were out of sight, and so were his hands and arms. What on earth was the man doing? The oil dipstick was on the other side. I rapped on the windshield. He seemed not to hear me. I put my head out of the window and shouted, 'Hey! Come out of there!'

Slowly, he straightened up, and as he drew his right arm out of the bowels of the engine, I saw that he was holding in his fingers something that was long and black and curly and very thin.

'Good God!' I thought. 'He's found a snake in there!'

He came round to the window, grinning at me and holding the object out for me to see; and only then, as I got a closer look, did I realize that it was not a snake at all – *it was the fan-belt of my Lagonda*!

All the awful implications of suddenly being stranded in this outlandish place with this disgusting man came flooding over me as I sat there staring dumbly at my broken fan-belt.

'You can see,' the Arab was saying, 'it was hanging on by a single thread. A good thing I noticed it.'

I took it from him and examined it closely. 'You cut it!' I cried.

'Cut it?' he answered softly. 'Why should I cut it?'

To be perfectly honest, it was impossible for me to judge whether he had or had not cut it. If he had, then he had also taken the trouble to fray the severed ends with some instrument to make it look like an ordinary break. Even so, my guess was that he *had* cut it, and if I was right then the implications were more sinister than ever.

'I suppose you know I can't go on without a fan-belt?' I said.

He grinned again with that awful mutilated mouth, showing ulcerated gums. 'If you go now,' he said, 'you will boil over in three minutes.'

'So what do you suggest?'

'I shall get you another fan-belt.'

'You will?'

'Of course. There is a telephone here, and if you will pay for the call, I will telephone to Ismailia. And if they haven't got one in Ismailia, I will telephone to Cairo. There is no problem.'

'No problem!' I shouted, getting out of the car. 'And when, pray, do you think the fan-belt is going to arrive in this ghastly place?'

'There is a mail-truck comes through every morning about ten o'clock. You would have it tomorrow.'

The man had all the answers. He never even had to think before replying.

This bastard, I thought, *has cut fan-belts before.*

I was very alert now, and watching him closely.

'They will not have a fan-belt for a machine of this make in Ismailia,' I said. 'It would have to come from the agents in Cairo. I will telephone them myself.' The fact that there was a telephone gave me some comfort. The telephone poles had followed the road all the way across the desert, and I could see the two wires leading into the hut from the nearest pole. 'I will ask the agents in Cairo to set out immediately for this place in a special vehicle,' I said.

The Arab looked along the road towards Cairo, some two hundred miles away. 'Who is going to drive six hours here and six hours back to bring a fan-belt?' he said. 'The mail will be just as quick.'

'Show me the telephone,' I said, starting towards the hut. Then a nasty thought struck me, and I stopped.

How could I possibly use this man's contaminated instrument? The earpiece would have to be pressed against my ear, and the mouthpiece would almost certainly touch my mouth; and I didn't give a damn what the doctors said about the impossibility of catching syphilis from remote contact. A syphilitic mouthpiece was a syphilitic mouthpiece, and you wouldn't catch *me* putting it anywhere near *my* lips, thank you very much. I wouldn't even enter his hut.

I stood there in the sizzling heat of the afternoon and looked at the Arab with his ghastly diseased face, and the Arab looked back at me, as cool and unruffled as you please.

'You want the telephone?' he asked.

'No,' I said. 'Can you read English?'

'Oh, yes.'

'Very well. I shall write down for you the name of the agents and the name of this car, and also my own name. They know me there. You will then tell them what is wanted. And listen . . . tell them to dispatch a special car immediately at my expense. I will pay them well. And if they won't do that, tell them they *have* to get the fan-belt to Ismailia in time to catch the mail-truck. You understand?'

'There is no problem,' the Arab said.

So I wrote down what was necessary on a piece of paper and gave it to him. He walked away with that slow, stamping tread towards the hut, and disappeared inside. I closed the bonnet of the car. Then I went back and sat in the driver's seat to think things out.

I poured myself another whisky, and lit a cigarette. There must be *some* traffic on this road. Somebody would surely come along before nightfall. But would that help me? No, it wouldn't – unless I were prepared to hitch a ride and leave the Lagonda and all my baggage behind to the tender mercies of the Arab. Was I prepared to do that? I didn't know. Probably yes. But if I were forced to stay the night, I would lock myself in the car and try to keep awake as much as possible. On no account would I enter the shack where that creature lived. Nor would I touch his food. I had whisky and water, and I had half a watermelon and a slab of chocolate. That was ample.

The heat was pretty bad. The thermometer in the car was still around 104°. It was hotter outside in the sun. I was perspiring freely. My God, what a place to get stranded in! And what a companion!

After about fifteen minutes, the Arab came out of the hut. I watched him all the way to the car.

'I talked to garage in Cairo,' he said, pushing his face through the window. 'Fan-belt will arrive tomorrow by mail-truck. Everything arranged.'

'Did you ask them about sending it at once?'

'They said impossible,' he answered.

'You're sure you asked them?'

He inclined his head to one side and gave me that sly insolent grin. I turned away and waited for him to go. He stayed where he was. 'We have house for visitors,' he said. 'You can sleep there very nice. My wife will make food, but you will have to pay.'

'Who else is here besides you and your wife?'

'Another man,' he said. He waved an arm in the direction of the three shacks across the road, and I turned and saw a man standing in the doorway of the middle shack, a short wide man who was dressed in dirty khaki slacks and shirt. He was standing absolutely motionless in the shadow of the doorway, his arms dangling at his sides. He was looking at me.

'Who is he?' I said.

'Saleh.'

'What does he do?'

'He helps.'

'I will sleep in the car,' I said. 'And it will not be necessary for your wife to prepare food. I have my own.' The Arab shrugged and turned away and started back towards the shack where the telephone was. I stayed in the car. What else could I do? It was just after two thirty. In three or four hours' time it would start to get a little cooler. Then I could take a stroll and maybe hunt up a few scorpions. Meanwhile, I had to make the best of things as they were. I reached into the back of the car where I kept my box of books and, without looking, I took out the first one I touched. The box contained thirty or forty of the best books in the world, and all of them could be reread a hundred times and would improve with each reading.

It was immaterial which one I got. It turned out to be *The Natural History of Selborne.* I opened it at random . . .

> . . . We had in this village more than twenty years ago an idiot boy, whom I well remember, who, from a child, showed a strong propensity to bees; they were his food, his amusement, his sole object. And as people of this cast have seldom more than one point of view, so this lad exerted all his few faculties on this one pursuit. In winter he dozed away his time, within his father's house, by the fireside, in a kind of torpid state, seldom departing from the chimney-corner; but in the summer he was all alert, and in quest of his game in the fields, and on sunny banks. Honey-bees, bumble-bees, wasps, were his prey wherever he found them; he had no apprehensions from their stings, but would seize them *nudis manibus*, and at once disarm them of their weapons, and suck their bodies for the sake of their honey-bags. Sometimes he would fill his bosom, between his shirt and his skin, with a number of these captives, and sometimes confine them to bottles. He was a very *merops apiaster*, or bee-bird, and very injurious to men that kept bees; for he would slide into their bee-gardens, and, sitting down before the stools, would rap with his fingers on the hives, and so take the bees as they came out. He has been known to overturn hives for the sake of honey, of which he is passionately fond. Where metheglin was making, he would linger around the tubs and vessels, begging a draught of what he called bee-wine. As he ran about, he used to make a humming noise with his lips, resembling the buzzing of bees . . .

I glanced up from the book and looked around me. The motionless man across the road had disappeared. There was nobody in sight. The silence was eerie, and the stillness, the utter stillness and desolation of the place was profoundly oppressive. I knew I was being watched. I knew that every little move I made, every sip of whisky and every puff of a cigarette, was being carefully noticed. I detest violence and I never carry a weapon. But I could have done with one now. For a while, I toyed with the idea of starting the motor and driving on down the road until the engine boiled over. But how far would I get? Not very far in this heat and without a fan. One mile, perhaps, or two at the most . . .

No – to hell with it. I would stay where I was and read my book.

It must have been about an hour later that I noticed a small dark speck moving towards me along the road in the far distance, coming from the Jerusalem direction. I laid aside my book without taking my eyes away from the speck. I watched it growing bigger and bigger. It was travelling at a great speed, at a really amazing speed. I got out of the Lagonda and hurried to the side of the road and stood there, ready to signal the driver to stop.

Closer and closer it came, and when it was about a quarter of a mile away, it began to slow down. Suddenly, I noticed the shape of its radiator. It was a *Rolls-Royce*! I raised an arm and kept it raised, and the big green car with a man at the wheel pulled in off the road and stopped beside my Lagonda.

I felt absurdly elated. Had it been a Ford or a Morris,

I would have been pleased enough, but I would not have been elated. The fact that it was a Rolls – a Bentley would have done equally well, or an Isotta, or another Lagonda – was a virtual guarantee that I would receive all the assistance I required; for whether you know it or not, there is a powerful brotherhood existing among people who own very costly automobiles. They respect one another automatically, and the reason they respect one another is simply that wealth respects wealth. In point of fact, there is nobody in the world that a very wealthy person respects more than another very wealthy person, and because of this, they naturally seek each other out wherever they go. Recognition signals of many kinds are used among them. With the female, the wearing of massive jewels is perhaps the most common; but the costly automobile is also much favoured, and is used by both sexes. It is a travelling placard, a public declaration of affluence, and as such, it is also a card of membership to that excellent unofficial society, the Very-Wealthy-People's Union. I am a member myself of long standing, and am delighted to be one. When I meet another member, as I was about to do now, I feel an immediate rapport. I respect him. We speak the same language. He is one of *us*. I had good reason, therefore, to be elated.

The driver of the Rolls climbed out and came towards me. He was a small dark man with olive skin, and he wore an immaculate white linen suit. Probably a Syrian, I thought. Just possibly a Greek. In the heat of the day he looked as cool as could be.

'Good afternoon,' he said. 'Are you having trouble?'

I greeted him, and then, bit by bit, I told him everything that had happened.

'My dear fellow,' he said in perfect English, 'but my *dear fellow*, how very distressing. What rotten luck. This is no place to get stranded in.'

'It isn't, is it?'

'And you say that a new fan-belt has definitely been ordered?'

'Yes,' I answered, 'if I can rely upon the proprietor of this establishment.'

The Arab, who had emerged from his shack almost before the Rolls had come to a stop, now joined us, and the stranger proceeded to question him swiftly in Arabic about the steps he had taken on my behalf. It seemed to me that the two knew each other pretty well, and it was clear that the Arab was in great awe of the new arrival. He was practically crawling along the ground in his presence.

'Well – that seems to be all right,' the stranger said at last, turning to me. 'But quite obviously you won't be able to move on from here until tomorrow morning. Where were you headed for?'

'Jerusalem,' I said. 'And I don't relish the idea of spending the night in this infernal spot.'

'I should say not, my dear man. That would be most uncomfortable.' He smiled at me, showing exceptionally white teeth. Then he took out a cigarette case, and offered me a cigarette. The case was gold, and on the outside of it there was a thin line of green jade inlaid diagonally from corner to corner. It was a beautiful thing. I accepted the cigarette. He lit it for me, then lit his own.

The stranger took a long pull at his cigarette, inhaling deeply. Then he tilted back his head and blew the smoke up into the sun. 'We shall both get heat-stroke if we stand around here much longer,' he said. 'Will you permit me to make a suggestion?'

'But of course.'

'I do hope you won't consider it presumptuous, coming from a complete stranger . . .'

'Please . . .'

'You can't possibly remain here, so I suggest you come back and stay the night in my house.'

There! The Rolls-Royce was smiling at the Lagonda – smiling at it as it would never have smiled at a Ford or a Morris!

'You mean in Ismailia?' I said.

'No, no,' he answered, laughing. 'I live just around the corner, just over there.' He waved a hand in the direction he had come from.

'But surely you were going to Ismailia? I wouldn't want you to change your plans on my behalf.'

'I wasn't going to Ismailia at all,' he said. 'I was coming down here to collect the mail. My house – and this may surprise you – is quite close to where we are standing. You see that mountain? That's Maghara. I'm immediately behind it.'

I looked at the mountain. It lay about ten miles to the north, a yellow rocky lump, perhaps two thousand feet high. 'Do you really mean that you have a house in the middle of all this . . . this wasteland?' I asked.

'You don't believe me?' he said, smiling.

'Of course I believe you,' I answered. 'Nothing surprises me any more. Except, perhaps,' and here I smiled back at him, 'except when I meet a stranger in the middle of the desert, and he treats me like a brother. I am overwhelmed by your offer.'

'Nonsense, my dear fellow. My motives are entirely selfish. Civilized company is not easy to come by in these parts. I am quite thrilled at the thought of having a guest for dinner. Permit me to introduce myself – Abdul Aziz.' He made a quick little bow.

'Oswald Cornelius,' I said. 'It is a great pleasure.' We shook hands.

'I live partly in Beirut,' he said.

'I live in Paris.'

'Charming. And now – shall we go? Are you ready?'

'But my car,' I said. 'Can I leave it here safely?'

'Have no fear about that. Omar is a friend of mine. He's not much to look at, poor chap, but he won't let you down if you're with me. And the other one, Saleh, is a good mechanic. He'll fit your new fan-belt when it arrives tomorrow. I'll tell him now.'

Saleh, the man from across the road, had walked over while we were talking. Mr Aziz gave him his instructions. He then spoke to both men about guarding the Lagonda. He was brief and incisive. Omar and Saleh stood bowing and scraping. I went across to the Lagonda to get a suitcase. I needed a change of clothes badly.

'Oh, by the way,' Mr Aziz called over to me, 'I usually put on a black tie for dinner.'

'Of course,' I murmured, quickly pushing back my first choice of suitcase and taking another.

'I do it for the ladies mostly. They seem to like dressing themselves up for dinner.'

I turned sharply and looked at him, but he was already getting into his car.

'Ready?' he said.

I took the suitcase and placed it in the back of the Rolls. Then I climbed into the front seat beside him, and we drove off.

During the drive, we talked casually about this and that. He told me that his business was in carpets. He had offices in Beirut and Damascus. His forefathers, he said, had been in the trade for hundreds of years.

I mentioned that I had a seventeenth-century Damascus carpet on the floor of my bedroom in Paris.

'You don't mean it!' he cried, nearly swerving off the road with excitement. 'Is it silk and wool, with the warp made entirely of silk? And has it got a ground of gold and silver threads?'

'Yes,' I said. 'Exactly.'

'But my dear fellow! You mustn't put a thing like that on the floor!'

'It is touched only by bare feet,' I said.

That pleased him. It seemed that he loved carpets almost as much as I loved the blue vases of Tchin-Hoa.

Soon we turned left off the tarred road on to a hard stony track and headed straight over the desert towards the mountain. 'This is my private driveway,' Mr Aziz said. 'It is five miles long.'

'You are even on the telephone,' I said, noticing the poles that branched off the main road to follow his private drive.

And then suddenly a queer thought struck me.

That Arab at the filling-station . . . he also was on the telephone . . .

Might not this, then, explain the fortuitous arrival of Mr Aziz?

Was it possible that my lonely host had devised a clever method of shanghai-ing travellers off the road in order to provide himself with what he called 'civilized company' for dinner? Had he, in fact, given the Arab standing instructions to immobilize the cars of all likely-looking persons one after the other as they came along? 'Just cut the fan-belt, Omar. Then phone me up quick. But make sure it's a decent-looking fellow with a good car. Then I'll pop along and see if I think he's worth inviting to the house . . .'

It was ridiculous, of course.

'I think,' my companion was saying, 'that you are wondering why in the world I should choose to have a house out here in a place like this.'

'Well, yes. I am a bit.'

'Everyone does,' he said.

'*Everyone*,' I said.

'Yes,' he said.

Well, well, I thought – everyone.

'I live here,' he said, 'because I have a peculiar affinity

with the desert. I am drawn to it the same way as a sailor is drawn to the sea. Does that seem so very strange to you?'

'No,' I answered, 'it doesn't seem strange at all.'

He paused and took a pull at his cigarette. Then he said, 'That is one reason. But there is another. Are you a family man, Mr Cornelius?'

'Unfortunately not,' I answered cautiously.

'I am,' he said. 'I have a wife and a daughter. Both of them, in my eyes at any rate, are very beautiful. My daughter is just eighteen. She has been to an excellent boarding-school in England, and she is now . . .' he shrugged . . . 'she is now just sitting around and waiting until she is old enough to get married. But this waiting period – what does one do with a beautiful young girl during that time? I can't let her loose. She is far too desirable for that. When I take her to Beirut, I see the men hanging around her like wolves waiting to pounce. It drives me nearly out of my mind. I know all about men, Mr Cornelius. I know how they behave. It is true, of course, that I am not the only father who has had this problem. But the others seem somehow able to face it and accept it. They let their daughters go. They just turn them out of the house and look the other way. I cannot do that. I simply *cannot bring* myself to do it! I refuse to allow her to be mauled by every Achmed, Ali and Hamil that comes along. And that, you see, is the other reason why I live in the desert – to protect my lovely child for a few more years from the wild beasts. Did you say that you had no family at all, Mr Cornelius?'

'I'm afraid that's true.'

'Oh.' He seemed disappointed. 'You mean you've never been married?'

'Well . . . no,' I said. 'No, I haven't.' I waited for the next inevitable question. It came about a minute later.

'Have you never *wanted* to get married and have children?'

They all asked that one. It was simply another way of saying, 'Are you, in that case, homosexual?'

'Once,' I said. 'Just once.'

'What happened?'

'There was only one person ever in my life, Mr Aziz . . . and after she went . . .' I sighed.

'You mean she died?'

I nodded, too choked up to answer.

'My dear fellow,' he said. 'Oh, I am so sorry. Forgive me for intruding.'

We drove on for a while in silence.

'It's amazing,' I murmured, 'how one loses all interest in matters of the flesh after a thing like that. I suppose it's the shock. One never gets over it.'

He nodded sympathetically, swallowing it all.

'So now I just travel around trying to forget. I've been doing it for years . . .'

We had reached the foot of Mount Maghara now and were following the track as it curved round the mountain towards the side that was invisible from the road – the north side. 'As soon as we round the next bend you'll see the house,' Mr Aziz said.

We rounded the bend . . . and there it was! I blinked

and stared, and I tell you that for the first few seconds I literally could not believe my eyes. I saw before me a white castle – I mean it – a *tall, white castle* with turrets and towers and little spires all over it, standing like a fairy-tale in the middle of a small splash of green vegetation on the lower slope of the blazing-hot, bare, yellow mountain! It was fantastic! It was straight out of Hans Christian Andersen or Grimm. I had seen plenty of romantic-looking Rhine and Loire valley castles in my time, but never before had I seen anything with such a slender, graceful, fairy-tale quality as this! The greenery, as I observed when we drew closer, was a pretty garden of lawns and date-palms, and there was a high white wall going all the way round to keep out the desert.

'Do you approve?' my host asked, smiling.

'It's fabulous!' I said. 'It's like all the fairy-tale castles in the world made into one.'

'That's exactly what it is!' he cried. 'It's a fairy-tale castle! I built it especially for my daughter, my beautiful Princess.'

And the beautiful Princess is imprisoned within its walls by her strict and jealous father, King Abdul Aziz, who refuses to allow her the pleasures of masculine company. But watch out, for here comes Prince Oswald Cornelius to the rescue! Unbeknownst to the King, he is going to ravish the beautiful Princess, and make her very happy.

'You have to admit it's different,' Mr Aziz said.

'It is that.'

'It is also nice and private. I sleep very peacefully here. So does the Princess. No unpleasant young men are likely to come climbing in through *those* windows during the night.'

'Quite so,' I said.

'It used to be a small oasis,' he went on. 'I bought it from the government. We have ample water for the house, the swimming-pool and three acres of garden.'

We drove through the main gates, and I must say it was wonderful to come suddenly into a miniature paradise of green lawns and flowerbeds and palm trees. Everything was in perfect order, and water-sprinklers were playing on the lawns. When we stopped at the front door of the house, two servants in spotless gallabiyahs and scarlet tarbooshes ran out immediately, one to each side of the car, to open the doors for us.

Two servants? But would both of them have come out like that unless they'd been expecting *two* people? I doubted it. More and more, it began to look as though my odd little theory about being shanghaied as a dinner guest was turning out to be correct. It was all very amusing.

My host ushered me in through the front door, and at once I got that lovely shivery feeling that comes over the skin as one walks suddenly out of intense heat into an air-conditioned room. I was standing in the hall. The floor was of green marble. On my right, there was a wide archway leading to a large room, and I received a fleeting impression of cool white walls, fine pictures and superlative Louis XV furniture. What a place to find oneself in, in the middle of the Sinai Desert!

And now a woman was coming slowly down the stairs. My host had turned away to speak to the servants, and he didn't see her at once, so when she reached the bottom step, the woman paused, and she laid her naked arm like a white anaconda along the rail of the banister, and there she stood, looking at me as though she were Queen Semiramis on the steps of Babylon, and I was a candidate who might or might not be to her taste. Her hair was jet-black, and she had a figure that made me wet my lips.

When Mr Aziz turned and saw her, he said, 'Oh darling, there you are. I've brought you a guest. His car broke down at the filling-station – such rotten luck – so I asked him to come back and stay the night. Mr Cornelius . . . my wife.'

'How very nice,' she said quietly, coming forward.

I took her hand and raised it to my lips. 'I am overcome by your kindness, madame,' I murmured. There was, upon that hand of hers, a diabolical perfume. It was almost exclusively animal. The subtle, sexy secretions of the sperm-whale, the male musk-deer and the beaver were all there, pungent and obscene beyond words; they dominated the blend completely, and only faint traces of the clean vegetable oils – lemon, cajuput and zeroli – were allowed to come through. It was superb! And another thing I noticed in the flash of that first moment was this: when I took her hand, she did not, as other women do, let it lie limply across my palm like a fillet of raw fish. Instead, she placed her thumb *underneath* my hand, with the fingers on top; and thus she was able to – and I swear she did – exert a gentle but suggestive pressure upon my hand as I administered the conventional kiss.

'Where is Diana?' asked Mr Aziz.

'She's out by the pool,' the woman said. And turning to me, 'Would *you* like a swim, Mr Cornelius? You must be roasted after hanging around that awful filling-station.'

She had huge velvet eyes, so dark they were almost black, and when she smiled at me, the end of her nose moved upwards, distending the nostrils.

There and then, Prince Oswald Cornelius decided that he cared not one whit about the beautiful Princess who was held captive in the castle by the jealous King. He would ravish the Queen instead.

'Well . . .' I said.

'I'm going to have one,' Mr Aziz said.

'Let's all have one,' his wife said. 'We'll lend you a pair of trunks.'

I asked if I might go up to my room first and get out a clean shirt and clean slacks to put on after the swim, and my hostess said, 'Yes, of course,' and told one of the servants to show me the way. He took me up two flights of stairs, and we entered a large white bedroom which had in it an exceptionally large double-bed. There was a well-equipped bathroom leading off to one side, with a pale-blue bathtub and a bidet to match. Everywhere, things were scrupulously clean and very much to my liking. While the servant was unpacking my case, I went over to the window and looked out, and I saw the great blazing desert sweeping in like a yellow sea all the way from the horizon until it met the white garden wall just below me, and there, within the wall, I could see the swimming-pool, and beside the pool there was a girl lying on her back in the shade of a big pink parasol. The girl was wearing a white swimming-costume, and she was reading a book. She had long slim legs and black hair. She was the Princess.

What a set-up, I thought. The white castle, the comfort, the cleanliness, the air-conditioning, the two dazzlingly beautiful females, the watchdog husband, and a whole evening to work in! The situation was so perfectly designed for my entertainment that it would have been impossible to improve upon it. The problems that lay ahead appealed to me very much. A simple straightforward seduction did not amuse me any more. There was no artistry in that sort of thing; and I can assure you that had I been able, by waving a magic wand, to make Mr Abdul Aziz, the jealous watchdog, disappear for the night, I would not have done so. I wanted no pyrrhic victories.

When I left the room, the servant accompanied me. We descended the first flight of stairs, and then, on the landing of the floor below my own, I paused and said casually, 'Does the whole family sleep on this floor?'

'Oh, yes,' the servant said. 'That is the master's room there' – indicating a door – 'and next to it is Mrs Aziz. Miss Diana is opposite.'

Three separate rooms. All very close together. Virtually impregnable. I tucked the information away in my mind and went on down to the pool. My host and hostess were there before me.

'This is my daughter, Diana,' my host said.

The girl in the white swimming-suit stood up and I kissed her hand. 'Hello, Mr Cornelius,' she said.

She was using the same heavy animal perfume as her mother – ambergris, musk and castor! What a smell it had – bitchy, brazen and marvellous! I sniffed at it like a dog. She was, I thought, even more beautiful than the parent, if that were possible. She had the same large velvety eyes, the same black hair, and the same shape of face; but her legs were unquestionably longer, and there was something about her body that gave it a slight edge over the older woman's: it was more sinuous, more snaky and almost certain to be a good deal more flexible. But the older woman, who was probably thirty-seven and looked no more than twenty-five, had a spark in her eye that her daughter could not possibly match.

Eeny, meeny, miny, mo – just a little while ago, Prince Oswald had sworn that he would ravish the Queen alone, and to hell with the Princess. But now that he had seen the Princess in the flesh, he did not know which one to prefer. Both of them, in their different ways, held forth a promise of innumerable delights, the one innocent and eager, the other expert and voracious. The truth of the matter was that he would like to have them both – the Princess as an hors d'œuvre, and the Queen as the main dish.

'Help yourself to a pair of trunks in the changing-room, Mr Cornelius,' Mrs Aziz was saying, so I went into the hut and changed, and when I came out again the three of them were already splashing about in the water. I dived in and joined them. The water was so cold it made me gasp.

'I thought that would surprise you,' Mr Aziz said, laughing. 'It's cooled. I keep it at sixty-five degrees. It's more refreshing in this climate.'

Later, when the sun began dropping lower in the sky, we all sat around in our wet swimming-clothes while a servant brought us pale, ice-cold martinis, and it was at this point that I began, very slowly, very cautiously, to seduce the two ladies in my own particular fashion. Normally, when I am given a free hand, this is not especially difficult for me to do. The curious little talent that I happen to possess – the ability to hypnotize a woman with words – very seldom lets me down. It is not, of course, done only with words. The words themselves, the innocuous, superficial words, are spoken only by the mouth, whereas the real message, the improper and exciting promise, comes from all the limbs and organs of the body, and is transmitted through the eyes. More than that I cannot honestly tell you about how it is done. The point is that it works. It works like cantharides. I believe that I could sit down opposite the Pope's wife, if he had one, and within fifteen minutes, were I to try hard enough, she would be leaning towards me over the table with her lips apart and her eyes glazed with desire. It is a minor talent, not a great one, but I am none the less thankful to have had it bestowed upon me, and I have done my best at all times to see that it has not been wasted.

So the four of us, the two wondrous women, the little man and myself, sat close together in a semicircle beside the swimming-pool, lounging in deck-chairs and sipping our drinks and feeling the warm six o'clock sunshine upon our skin. I was in good form. I made them laugh a great deal. The story about the greedy old Duchess of Glasgow putting her hand in the chocolate box and getting nipped by one of my scorpions had the daughter falling out of her chair with mirth; and when I described in detail the interior of my spider breeding-house in the garden outside Paris, both ladies began wriggling with revulsion and pleasure.

It was at this stage that I noticed the eyes of Mr Abdul

Aziz resting upon me in a good-humoured, twinkling kind of way. 'Well, well,' the eyes seemed to be saying, 'we are glad to see that you are not quite so disinterested in women as you led us to believe in the car . . . Or is it, perhaps, that these congenial surroundings are helping you to forget that great sorrow of yours at last . . .' Mr Aziz smiled at me, showing his pure white teeth. It was a friendly smile. I gave him a friendly smile back. What a friendly little fellow he was. He was genuinely delighted to see me paying so much attention to the ladies. So far, then, so good.

I shall skip very quickly over the next few hours, for it was not until after midnight that anything really tremendous happened to me. A few brief notes will suffice to cover the intervening period:

At seven o'clock, we all left the swimming-pool and returned to the house to dress for dinner.

At eight o'clock, we assembled in the big living-room to drink another cocktail. The two ladies were both superbly turned out, and sparkling with jewels. Both of them wore low-cut, sleeveless evening-dresses which had come, without any doubt at all, from some great fashion house in Paris. My hostess was in black, her daughter in pale blue, and the scent of that intoxicating perfume was everywhere about them. What a pair they were! The older woman had that slight forward hunch to her shoulders which one sees only in the most passionate and practised of females; for in the same way as a horsey woman will become bandy-legged from sitting constantly upon a horse, so a woman of great passion will develop a curious roundness of the shoulders from continually embracing men. It is an occupational deformity, and the noblest of them all.

The daughter was not yet old enough to have acquired this singular badge of honour, but with her it was enough for me simply to stand back and observe the shape of her body and to notice the splendid sliding motion of her thighs underneath the tight silk dress as she wandered about the room. She had a line of tiny soft golden hairs growing all the way up the exposed length of her spine, and when I stood behind her it was difficult to resist the temptation of running my knuckles up and down those lovely vertebrae.

At eight thirty, we moved into the dining-room. The dinner that followed was a really magnificent affair, but I shall waste no time here describing food or wine. Throughout the meal I continued to play most delicately and insidiously upon the sensibilities of the women, employing every skill that I possessed; and by the time the dessert arrived, they were melting before my eyes like butter in the sun.

After dinner we returned to the living-room for coffee and brandy, and then, at my host's suggestion, we played a couple of rubbers of bridge.

By the end of the evening, I knew for certain that I had done my work well. The old magic had not let me down. Either of the two ladies, should circumstances permit, was mine for the asking. I was not deluding myself over this. It was a straightforward, obvious fact. It stood out a mile. The face of my hostess was bright with excitement, and whenever she looked at me across the card table, those huge dark velvety eyes would grow bigger and bigger, and the nostrils would dilate, and the mouth would open slightly to reveal the tip of a moist pink tongue squeezing through between the teeth. It was a marvellously lascivious gesture, and more than once it caused me to trump my own trick. The daughter was less daring but equally direct. Each time her eyes met mine, and that was often enough, she would raise her brows just the tiniest fraction of a centimetre, as though asking a question; then she would make a quick sly little smile, supplying the answer.

'I think it's time we all went to bed,' Mr Aziz said, examining his watch. 'It's after eleven. Come along, my dears.'

Then a queer thing happened. At once, without a second's hesitation and without another glance in my direction, both ladies rose and made for the door! It was astonishing. It left me stunned. I didn't know what to make of it. It was the quickest thing I'd ever seen. And yet it wasn't as though Mr Aziz had spoken angrily. His voice, to me at any rate, had sounded as pleasant as ever. But now he was already turning out the lights, indicating clearly that he wished me also to retire. What a blow! I had expected at least to receive a whisper from either the wife or the daughter before we separated for the night, just a quick three or four words telling me where to go and when; but instead, I was left standing like a fool beside the card table while the two ladies glided out of the room.

My host and I followed them up the stairs. On the landing of the first floor, the mother and daughter stood side by side, waiting for me.

'Goodnight, Mr Cornelius,' my hostess said.

'Goodnight, Mr Cornelius,' the daughter said.

'Goodnight, my dear fellow,' Mr Aziz said. 'I do hope you have everything you want.'

They turned away, and there was nothing for me to do but continue slowly, reluctantly, up the second flight of stairs to my own room. I entered it and closed the door. The heavy brocade curtains had already been drawn by one of the servants, but I parted them and leaned out of the window to take a look at the night. The air was still and warm, and a brilliant moon was shining over the desert. Below me, the swimming-pool in the moonlight looked something like an enormous glass mirror lying flat on the lawn, and beside it I could see the four deck-chairs we had been sitting in earlier.

Well, well, I thought. What happens now?

One thing I knew I must not do in this house was to venture out of my room and go prowling around the corridors. That would be suicide. I had learned many years ago that there are three breeds of husband with whom one must never take unnecessary risks – the Bulgarian, the Greek and the Syrian. None of them, for some reason, resents you flirting quite openly with his wife, but he will kill you at once if he catches you getting into her bed. Mr Aziz was a Syrian. A degree of prudence was therefore essential, and if any move were going to be made now, it must be made not by me but by one of the two women, for only she (or they) would know precisely what was safe and what was dangerous. Yet I had to admit that after witnessing the way in which my host had called them both to heel four minutes ago, there was very little hope of further action in the near future. The trouble was, though, that I had gotten myself so infernally steamed up.

I undressed and took a long cold shower. That helped. Then, because I have never been able to sleep in the moonlight, I made sure that the curtains were tightly drawn together. I got into bed, and for the next hour or so I lay reading some more of Gilbert White's *Natural History of Selborne.* That also helped, and at last, somewhere between midnight and one a.m., there came a time when I was able to switch out the light and prepare myself for sleep without altogether too many regrets.

I was just beginning to doze off when I heard some tiny sounds. I recognized them at once. They were sounds that I had heard many times before in my life, and yet they were still, for me, the most thrilling and evocative in the whole world. They consisted of a series of little soft metallic noises, of metal grating gently against metal, and they were made, they were always made by somebody who was very slowly, very cautiously, turning the handle of one's door from the outside. Instantly, I became wide awake. But I did not move. I simply opened my eyes and stared in the direction of the door; and I can remember wishing at that moment for a gap in the curtain, for just a small thin shaft of moonlight to come in from outside so that I could at least catch a glimpse of the shadow of the lovely form that was about to enter. But the room was as dark as a dungeon.

I did not hear the door open. No hinge squeaked. But suddenly a little gust of air swept through the room and rustled the curtains and a moment later I heard the soft thud of wood against wood as the door was carefully closed again. Then came the click of the latch as the handle was released.

Next, I heard feet tiptoeing towards me over the carpet.

For one horrible second, it occurred to me that this might just possibly be Mr Abdul Aziz creeping in upon me with a long knife in his hand, but then all at once a warm extensile body was bending over mine, and a woman's voice was whispering in my ear, '*Don't make a sound!*'

'My dearest beloved,' I said, wondering which one of them it was, 'I knew you'd . . .' Instantly her hand came over my mouth.

'*Please!*' she whispered. '*Not another word!*'

I didn't argue. My lips had many better things to do than that. So had hers.

Here I must pause. This is not like me at all – I know that. But just for once, I wish to be excused a detailed description of the great scene that followed. I have my own reasons for this and I beg you to respect them. In any case, it will do you no harm to exercise your own imagination for a change, and if you wish, I will stimulate it a little by saying simply and truthfully that of the many thousands and thousands of women I have known in my time, none has transported me to greater extremes of ecstasy than this lady of the Sinai Desert. Her dexterity was amazing. Her passion was intense. Her range was unbelievable. At every turn, she was ready with some new and intricate manoeuvre. And to cap it all, she possessed the subtlest and most recondite style I have ever encountered. She was a great artist. She was a genius.

All this, you will probably say, indicated clearly that my visitor must have been the older woman. You would be wrong. It indicated nothing. True genius is a gift of birth. It has very little to do with age; and I can assure you I had no way of knowing for certain which of them it was in the darkness of that room. I wouldn't have bet a penny on it either way. At one moment, after some particularly boisterous cadenza, I would be convinced it was the wife. *It must be the wife!* Then suddenly the whole tempo would begin to change, and the melody would become so childlike and innocent that I found myself swearing it was the daughter. *It must be the daughter!*

Maddening it was not to know the true answer. It tantalized me. It also humbled me, for, after all, a connoisseur, a supreme connoisseur, should always be able to guess the vintage without seeing the label on the bottle. But this one really had me beat. At one point, I reached for cigarettes, intending to solve the mystery in the flare of a match, but her hand was on me in a flash, and cigarettes and matches both were snatched away and flung across the room. More than once, I began to whisper the question itself into her ear, but I never got three words out before the hand shot up again and smacked itself over my mouth. Rather violently, too.

Very well, I thought. Let it be for now. Tomorrow morning, downstairs in the daylight, I shall know by the glow on the face, by the way the eyes look back into mine, and by a hundred other little tell-tale signs. I shall also know by the marks that my teeth have made on the left side of the neck, above the dress line. A rather wily move, that one, I thought, and so perfectly timed – my vicious bite was administered during the height of her passion – that she never for one moment realized the significance of the act.

It was altogether a most memorable night, and at least four hours must have gone by before she gave me a final fierce embrace, and slipped out of the room as quickly as she had come in.

The next morning I did not awaken until after ten o'clock. I got out of bed and drew open the curtains. It was another brilliant, hot, desert day. I took a leisurely bath, then dressed myself as carefully as ever. I felt relaxed and chipper. It made me very happy to think that I could still summon a woman to my room with my eyes alone, even in middle-age. And what a woman! It would be fascinating to find out which one of them she was. I would soon know.

I made my way slowly down the two flights of stairs.

'Good morning, my dear fellow, good morning!' Mr Aziz said, rising from a small desk he had been writing at in the living-room. 'Did you have a good night?'

'Excellent, thank you,' I answered, trying not to sound smug.

He came and stood close to me, smiling with his very white teeth. His shrewd little eyes rested on my face and moved over it slowly, as though searching for something.

'I have good news for you,' he said. 'They called up from B'ir Rawd Salim five minutes ago and said your new fan-belt had arrived by the mail-truck. Saleh is fitting it on now. It'll be ready in an hour. So when you've had some breakfast, I'll drive you over and you can be on your way.'

I told him how grateful I was.

'We'll be sorry to see you go,' he said. 'It's been an immense pleasure for all of us having you drop in like this, an immense pleasure.'

I had my breakfast alone in the dining-room. Afterwards, I returned to the living-room to smoke a cigarette while my host continued writing at his desk.

'Do forgive me,' he said. 'I just have a couple of things to finish here. I won't be long. I've arranged for your case to be packed and put in the car, so you have nothing to worry about. Sit down and enjoy your cigarette. The ladies ought to be down any minute now.'

The wife arrived first. She came sailing into the room looking more than ever like the dazzling Queen Semiramis of the Nile, and the first thing I noticed about her was the pale-green chiffon scarf knotted casually round her neck! Casually but carefully! So carefully that no part of the skin of the neck was visible. The woman went straight over to her husband and kissed him on the cheek. 'Good morning, my darling,' she said.

You cunning beautiful bitch, I thought.

'Good *morning*, Mr Cornelius,' she said gaily, coming over to sit in the chair opposite mine. 'Did you have a good night? I do hope you had everything you wanted.'

Never in my life have I seen such a sparkle in a woman's eyes as I saw in hers that morning, nor such a glow of pleasure in a woman's face.

'I had a very good night indeed, thank *you*,' I answered, showing her that I knew.

She smiled and lit a cigarette. I glanced over at Mr Aziz,

who was still writing away busily at the desk with his back to us. He wasn't paying the slightest attention to his wife or to me. He was, I thought, exactly like all the other poor cuckolds that I had ever created. Not one of them would believe that it could happen to him, not right under his own nose.

'Good morning, everybody!' cried the daughter, sweeping into the room. 'Good morning, Daddy! Good morning, Mummy!' She gave them each a kiss. 'Good morning, Mr Cornelius!' She was wearing a pair of pink slacks and a rust-coloured blouse, and I'll be damned if she didn't also have a scarf tied carelessly but carefully round her neck! A chiffon scarf!

'Did you have a decent night?' she asked, perching herself like a young bride on the arm of my chair, arranging herself in such a way that one of her thighs rested against my forearm. I leaned back and looked at her closely. She looked back at me and winked. She actually winked! Her face was glowing and sparkling every bit as much as her mother's, and if anything, she seemed even more pleased with herself than the older woman.

I felt pretty confused. Only one of them had a bite mark to conceal, yet both of them had covered their necks with scarves. I conceded that this might be a coincidence, but on the face of it, it looked much more like a conspiracy to me. It looked as though they were both working closely together to keep me from discovering the truth. But what an extraordinarily screwy business! And what was the purpose of it all? And in what other peculiar ways, might I ask, did they plot and plan together among themselves? Had they drawn lots or something the night before? Or did they simply take it in turns with visitors? I *must* come back again, I told myself, for another visit as soon as possible just to see what happens the next time. In fact, I might motor down specially from Jerusalem in a day or two. It would be easy, I reckoned, to get myself invited again.

'Are you ready, Mr Cornelius?' Mr Aziz said, rising from his desk.

'Quite ready,' I answered.

The ladies, sleek and smiling, led the way outside to where the big green Rolls-Royce was waiting. I kissed their hands and murmured a million thanks to each of them. Then I got into the front seat beside my host, and we drove off. The mother and daughter waved. I lowered my window and waved back. Then we were out of the garden and into the desert, following the stony yellow track as it skirted the base of Mount Maghara, with the telegraph poles marching along beside us.

During the journey, my host and I conversed pleasantly about this and that. I was at pains to be as agreeable as possible because my one object now was to get myself invited to stay at the house again. If I didn't succeed in getting *him* to ask *me*, then I should have to ask *him*. I would do it at the last moment. 'Good-bye, my dear friend,' I would say, gripping him warmly by the throat. 'May I have the pleasure of dropping in to see you again if I happen to be passing this way?' And of course he would say yes.

'Did you think I exaggerated when I told you my daughter was beautiful?' he asked me.

'You understated it,' I said. 'She's a raving beauty. I do congratulate you. But your wife is no less lovely. In fact, between the two of them they almost swept me off my feet,' I added, laughing.

'I noticed that,' he said, laughing with me. 'They're a couple of very naughty girls. They do so love to flirt with other men. But why should I mind? There's no harm in flirting.'

'None whatsoever,' I said.

'I think it's gay and fun.'

'It's charming,' I said.

In less than half an hour we had reached the main Ismailia–Jerusalem road. Mr Aziz turned the Rolls on to the black tarmac strip and headed for the filling-station at seventy miles an hour. In a few minutes we would be there. So now I tried moving a little closer to the subject of another visit, fishing gently for an invitation. 'I can't get over your house,' I said. 'I think it's simply wonderful.'

'It is nice, isn't it?'

'I suppose you're bound to get pretty lonely out there, on and off, just the three of you together?'

'It's no worse than anywhere else,' he said. 'People get lonely wherever they are. A desert, or a city – it doesn't make much difference, really. But we do have visitors, you know. You'd be surprised at the number of people who drop in from time to time. Like you, for instance. It was a great pleasure having you with us, my dear fellow.'

'I shall never forget it,' I said. 'It is a rare thing to find kindness and hospitality of that order nowadays.'

I waited for him to tell me that I must come again, but he didn't. A little silence sprang up between us, a slightly uneasy little silence. To bridge it, I said, 'I think yours is the most thoughtful paternal gesture I've ever heard of in my life.'

'Mine?'

'Yes. Building a house right out there in the back of beyond and living in it just for your daughter's sake, to protect her. I think it's remarkable.'

I saw him smile, but he kept his eyes on the road and said nothing. The filling-station and the group of huts were now in sight about a mile ahead of us. The sun was high and it was getting hot inside the car.

'Not many fathers would put themselves out to that extent,' I went on.

Again he smiled, but somewhat bashfully this time, I thought. And then he said, 'I don't deserve *quite* as much credit as you like to give me, really I don't. To be absolutely honest with you, that pretty daughter of mine isn't the only reason for my living in such splendid isolation.'

'I know that.'

'You do?'

'You told me. You said the other reason was the desert. You loved it, you said, as a sailor loves the sea.'

'So I did. And it's quite true. But there's still a third reason.'

'Oh, and what is that?'

He didn't answer me. He sat quite still with his hands on the wheel and his eyes fixed on the road ahead.

'I'm sorry,' I said. 'I shouldn't have asked the question. It's none of my business.'

'No, no, that's quite all right,' he said. 'Don't apologize.'

I stared out of the window at the desert. 'I think it's hotter than yesterday,' I said. 'It must be well over a hundred already.'

'Yes.'

I saw him shifting a little in his seat, as though trying to get comfortable, and then he said, 'I don't really see why I shouldn't tell you the truth about that house. You don't strike me as being a gossip.'

'Certainly not,' I said.

We were close to the filling-station now, and he had slowed the car down almost to walking-speed to give himself time to say what he had to say. I could see the two Arabs standing beside my Lagonda, watching us.

'That daughter,' he said at length, 'the one you met – she isn't the only daughter I have.'

'Oh, really?'

'I've got another who is five years older than she.'

'And just as beautiful, no doubt,' I said. 'Where does she live? In Beirut?'

'No, she's in the house.'

'In which house? Not the one we've just left?'

'Yes.'

'But I never saw her!'

'Well,' he said, turning suddenly to watch my face, 'maybe not.'

'But why?'

'She has leprosy.'

I jumped.

'Yes, I know,' he said, 'it's a terrible thing. She has the worst kind, too, poor girl. It's called anaesthetic leprosy. It is highly resistant, and almost impossible to cure. If only it were the nodular variety, it would be much easier. But it isn't, and there you are. So when a visitor comes to the house, she keeps to her own apartment, on the third floor . . .'

The car must have pulled into the filling-station about then because the next thing I can remember was seeing Mr Abdul Aziz sitting there looking at me with those small clever black eyes of his, and he was saying, 'But my dear fellow, you mustn't alarm yourself like this. Calm yourself down, Mr Cornelius, calm yourself down! There's absolutely nothing in the world for you to worry about. It is not a very contagious disease. You have to have the most *intimate* contact with the person in order to catch it . . .'

I got out of the car very slowly and stood in the sunshine. The Arab with the diseased face was grinning at me and saying, 'Fan-belt all fixed now. Everything fine.' I reached into my pocket for cigarettes, but my hand was shaking so violently I dropped the packet on the ground. I bent down and retrieved it. Then I got a cigarette out and managed to light it. When I looked up again, I saw the green Rolls-Royce already half a mile down the road, and going away fast.

Mrs Bixby and the Colonel's Coat

First published in *Nugget* (1959)

America is the land of opportunity for women. Already they own about eighty-five per cent of the wealth of the nation. Soon they will have it all. Divorce has become a lucrative process, simple to arrange and easy to forget; and ambitious females can repeat it as often as they please and parlay their winnings to astronomical figures. The husband's death also brings satisfactory rewards and some ladies prefer to rely upon this method. They know that the waiting period will not be unduly protracted, for overwork and hypertension are bound to get the poor devil before long, and he will die at his desk with a bottle of benzedrines in one hand and a packet of tranquillizers in the other.

Succeeding generations of youthful American males are not deterred in the slightest by this terrifying pattern of divorce and death. The higher the divorce rate climbs, the more eager they become. Young men marry like mice, almost before they have reached the age of puberty, and a large proportion of them have at least two ex-wives on the payroll by the time they are thirty-six years old. To support these ladies in the manner to which they are accustomed, the men must work like slaves, which is of course precisely what they are. But now at last, as they approach their premature middle age, a sense of disillusionment and fear begins to creep slowly into their hearts, and in the evenings they take to huddling together in little groups, in clubs and bars, drinking their whiskies and swallowing their pills, and trying to comfort one another with stories.

The basic theme of these stories never varies. There are always three main characters – the husband, the wife and the dirty dog. The husband is a decent clean-living man, working hard at his job. The wife is cunning, deceitful and lecherous, and she is invariably up to some sort of jiggery-pokery with the dirty dog. The husband is too good a man even to suspect her. Things look black for the husband. Will the poor man ever find out? Must he be a cuckold for the rest of his life? Yes, he must. But wait! Suddenly, by a brilliant manoeuvre, the husband completely turns the tables on his monstrous spouse. The woman is flabbergasted, stupefied, humiliated, defeated. The audience of men around the bar smiles quietly to itself and takes a little comfort from the fantasy.

There are many of these stories going around, these wonderful wishful-thinking dreamworld inventions of the unhappy male, but most of them are too fatuous to be worth repeating, and far too fruity to be put down on paper. There is one, however, that seems to be superior to the rest, particularly as it has the merit of being true. It is extremely popular with twice- or thrice-bitten males in search of solace, and if you are one of them, and if you haven't heard it before, you may enjoy the way it comes out. The story is called 'Mrs Bixby and the Colonel's Coat', and it goes something like this:

Dr and Mrs Bixby lived in a smallish apartment somewhere in New York City. Dr Bixby was a dentist who made an average income. Mrs Bixby was a big vigorous woman with a wet mouth. Once a month, always on Friday afternoons, Mrs Bixby would board the train at Pennsylvania Station and travel to Baltimore to visit her old aunt. She would spend the night with the aunt and return to New York on the following day in time to cook supper for her husband. Dr Bixby accepted this arrangement good-naturedly. He knew that Aunt Maude lived in Baltimore, and that his wife was very fond of the old lady, and certainly it would be unreasonable to deny either of them the pleasure of a monthly meeting.

'Just so long as you don't ever expect me to accompany you,' Dr Bixby had said in the beginning.

'Of course not, darling,' Mrs Bixby had answered. 'After all, she is not *your* aunt. She's mine.'

So far so good.

At it turned out, however, the aunt was little more than a convenient alibi for Mrs Bixby. The dirty dog, in the shape of a gentleman known as the Colonel, was lurking slyly in the background, and our heroine spent the greater part of her Baltimore time in this scoundrel's company. The Colonel was exceedingly wealthy. He lived in a charming house on the outskirts of the town. No wife or family encumbered him, only a few discreet and loyal servants, and in Mrs Bixby's absence he consoled himself by riding his horses and hunting the fox.

Year after year, this pleasant alliance between Mrs Bixby and the Colonel continued without a hitch. They met so seldom – twelve times a year is not much when you come to think of it – that there was little or no chance of their growing bored with one another. On the contrary, the long wait between meetings only made the heart grow fonder, and each separate occasion became an exciting reunion.

'Tally-ho!' the Colonel would cry each time he met her at the station in the big car. 'My dear, I'd almost forgotten how ravishing you looked. Let's go to earth.'

Eight years went by.

It was just before Christmas, and Mrs Bixby was standing on the station in Baltimore waiting for the train to take her back to New York. This particular visit which had just ended had been more than usually agreeable, and she was in a cheerful mood. But then the Colonel's company always did that to her these days. The man had a way of making her feel that she was altogether a rather remarkable woman, a person of subtle and exotic talents, fascinating beyond measure; and what a very different thing that was from the dentist husband at home who never succeeded in making her feel that she was anything but a sort of eternal patient, someone who dwelt in the waiting-room, silent among the magazines, seldom if ever nowadays to be called in to suffer the finicky precise ministrations of those clean pink hands.

'The Colonel asked me to give you this,' a voice beside her said. She turned and saw Wilkins, the Colonel's groom, a small wizened dwarf with grey skin, and he was pushing a large flattish cardboard box into her arms.

'Good gracious me!' she cried, all of a flutter. 'My

heavens, what an enormous box! What is it, Wilkins? Was there a message? Did he send me a message?'

'No message,' the groom said, and he walked away.

As soon as she was on the train, Mrs Bixby carried the box into the privacy of the Ladies' Room and locked the door. How exciting this was! A Christmas present from the Colonel. She started to undo the string. 'I'll bet it's a dress,' she said aloud. 'It might even be two dresses. Or it might be a whole lot of beautiful underclothes. I won't look. I'll just feel around and try to guess what it is. I'll try to guess the colour as well, and exactly what it looks like. Also how much it cost.'

She shut her eyes tight and slowly lifted off the lid. Then she put one hand down into the box. There was some tissue paper on top; she could feel it and hear it rustling. There was also an envelope or a card of some sort. She ignored this and began burrowing underneath the tissue paper, the fingers reaching out delicately, like tendrils.

'My God,' she cried suddenly. 'It can't be true!'

She opened her eyes wide and stared at the coat. Then she pounced on it and lifted it out of the box. Thick layers of fur made a lovely noise against the tissue paper as they unfolded, and when she held it up and saw it hanging to its full length, it was so beautiful it took her breath away.

Never had she seen mink like this before. It *was* mink, wasn't it? Yes, of course it was. But what a glorious colour! The fur was almost pure black. At first she thought it *was* black; but when she held it closer to the window she saw that there was a touch of blue in it as well, a deep rich blue, like cobalt. Quickly she looked at the label. It said simply, WILD LABRADOR MINK. There was nothing else, no sign of where it had been bought or anything. But that, she told herself, was probably the Colonel's doing. The wily old fox was making darn sure he didn't leave any tracks. Good for him. But what in the world could it have cost? She hardly dared to think. Four, five, six thousand dollars? Possibly more.

She just couldn't take her eyes off it. Nor, for that matter, could she wait to try it on. Quickly she slipped off her own plain red coat. She was panting a little now, she couldn't help it, and her eyes were stretched very wide. But oh God, the feel of that fur! And those huge wide sleeves with their thick turned-up cuffs! Who was it had once told her that they always used female skins for the arms and male skins for the rest of the coat? Someone had told her that. Joan Rutfield, probably; though how *Joan* would know anything about *mink* she couldn't imagine.

The great black coat seemed to slide on to her almost of its own accord, like a second skin. Oh boy! It was the queerest feeling! She glanced into the mirror. It was fantastic. Her whole personality had suddenly changed completely. She looked dazzling, radiant, rich, brilliant, voluptuous, all at the same time. And the sense of power that it gave her! In this coat she could walk into any place she wanted and people would come scurrying around her like rabbits. The whole thing was just too wonderful for words!

Mrs Bixby picked up the envelope that was still lying in the box. She opened it and pulled out the Colonel's letter:

I once heard you saying you were fond of mink so I got you this. I'm told it's a good one. Please accept it with my sincere good wishes as a parting gift. For my own personal reasons I shall not be able to see you any more. Good-bye and good luck.

Well!

Imagine that!

Right out of the blue, just when she was feeling so happy.

No more Colonel.

What a dreadful shock.

She would miss him enormously.

Slowly, Mrs Bixby began stroking the lovely soft black fur of the coat. What you lose on the swings you get back on the roundabouts.

She smiled and folded the letter, meaning to tear it up and throw it out the window, but in folding it she noticed that there was something written on the other side:

P.S. Just tell them that nice generous aunt of yours gave it to you for Christmas.

Mrs Bixby's mouth, at that moment stretched wide in a silky smile, snapped back like a piece of elastic.

'The man must be mad!' she cried. 'Aunt Maude doesn't have that sort of money. She couldn't possibly give me this.'

But if Aunt Maude didn't give it to her, then who did?

Oh God! In the excitement of finding the coat and trying it on, she had completely overlooked this vital aspect.

In a couple of hours she would be in New York. Ten minutes after that she would be home, and the husband would be there to greet her; and even a man like Cyril, dwelling as he did in a dark phlegmy world of root canals, bicuspids and caries, would start asking a few questions if his wife suddenly waltzed in from a week-end wearing a six-thousand-dollar mink coat.

You know what I think, she told herself. I think that goddam Colonel has done this on purpose just to torture me. He knew perfectly well Aunt Maude didn't have enough money to buy this. He knew I wouldn't be able to keep it.

But the thought of parting with it now was more than Mrs Bixby could bear.

'I've *got* to have this coat!' she said aloud. 'I've got to have this coat! I've got to have this coat!'

Very well, my dear. You shall have the coat. But don't panic. Sit still and keep calm and start thinking. You're a clever girl, aren't you? You've fooled him before. The man never has been able to see much further than the end of his own probe, you know that. So just sit absolutely still and *think*. There's lots of time.

Two and a half hours later, Mrs Bixby stepped off the train at Pennsylvania Station and walked quickly to the exit. She was wearing her old red coat again now and carrying the cardboard box in her arms. She signalled for a taxi.

'Driver,' she said, 'would you know of a pawnbroker that's still open around here?'

The man behind the wheel raised his brows and looked back at her, amused.

'Plenty along Sixth Avenue,' he answered.

'Stop at the first one you see, then, will you please?' She got in and was driven away.

Soon the taxi pulled up outside a shop that had three brass balls hanging over the entrance.

'Wait for me, please,' Mrs Bixby said to the driver, and she got out of the taxi and entered the shop.

There was an enormous cat crouching on the counter eating fishheads out of a white saucer. The animal looked up at Mrs Bixby with bright yellow eyes, then looked away again and went on eating. Mrs Bixby stood by the counter, as far away from the cat as possible, waiting for someone to come, staring at the watches, the shoe buckles, the enamel brooches, the old binoculars, the broken spectacles, the false teeth. Why did they always pawn their teeth, she wondered.

'Yes?' the proprietor said, emerging from a dark place in the back of the shop.

'Oh, good evening,' Mrs Bixby said. She began to untie the string round the box. The man went up to the cat and started stroking it along the top of its back, and the cat went on eating the fishheads.

'Isn't it silly of me?' Mrs Bixby said. 'I've gone and lost my pocketbook, and this being Saturday, the banks are all closed until Monday and I've simply got to have some money for the week-end. This is quite a valuable coat, but I'm not asking much. I only want to borrow enough on it to tide me over till Monday. Then I'll come back and redeem it.'

The man waited, and said nothing. But when she pulled

out the mink and allowed the beautiful thick fur to fall over the counter, his eyebrows went up and he drew his hand away from the cat and came over to look at it. He picked it up and held it out in front of him.

'If only I had a watch on me or a ring,' Mrs Bixby said, 'I'd give you that instead. But the fact is I don't have a thing with me other than this coat.' She spread out her fingers for him to see.

'It looks new,' the man said, fondling the soft fur.

'Oh yes, it is. But, as I said, I only want to borrow enough to tide me over till Monday. How about fifty dollars?'

'I'll loan you fifty dollars.'

'It's worth a hundred times more than that, but I know you'll take good care of it until I return.'

The man went over to a drawer and fetched a ticket and placed it on the counter. The ticket looked like one of those labels you tie on to the handle of your suitcase, the same shape and size exactly, and the same stiff brownish paper. But it was perforated across the middle so that you could tear it in two, and both halves were identical.

'Name?' he asked.

'Leave that out. And the address.'

She saw the man pause, and she saw the nib of the pen hovering over the dotted line, waiting.

'You don't *have* to put the name and address, do you?'

The man shrugged and shook his head and the pen-nib moved on down to the next line.

'It's just that I'd rather not,' Mrs Bixby said. 'It's purely personal.'

'You'd better not lose this ticket, then.'

'I won't lose it.'

'You realize that anyone who gets hold of it can come in and claim the article?'

'Yes, I know that.'

'Simply on the number.'

'Yes, I know.'

'What do you want me to put for a description?'

'No description either, thank you. It's not necessary. Just put the amount I'm borrowing.'

The pen-nib hesitated again, hovering over the dotted line beside the word ARTICLE.

'I think you ought to put a description. A description is always a help if you want to sell the ticket. You never know, you might want to sell it sometime.'

'I don't want to sell it.'

'You might have to. Lots of people do.'

'Look,' Mrs Bixby said. 'I'm not broke, if that's what you mean. I simply lost my purse. Don't you understand?'

'You have it your own way then,' the man said. 'It's your coat.'

At this point an unpleasant thought struck Mrs Bixby. 'Tell me something,' she said. 'If I don't have a description on my ticket, how can I be sure you'll give me back the coat and not something else when I return?'

'It goes in the books.'

'But all I've got is a number. So actually you could hand me any old thing you wanted, isn't that so?'

'Do you want a description or don't you?' the man asked.

'No,' she said. 'I trust you.'

The man wrote 'fifty dollars' opposite the word VALUE on both sections of the ticket, then he tore it in half along the perforations and slid the lower portion across the counter. He took a wallet from the inside pocket of his jacket and extracted five ten-dollar bills. 'The interest is three per cent a month,' he said.

'Yes, all right. And thank you. You'll take good care of it, won't you?'

The man nodded but said nothing.

'Shall I put it back in the box for you?'

'No,' the man said.

Mrs Bixby turned and went out of the shop on to the street where the taxi was waiting. Ten minutes later, she was home.

'Darling,' she said as she bent over and kissed her husband. 'Did you miss me?'

Cyril Bixby laid down the evening paper and glanced at the watch on his wrist. 'It's twelve and a half minutes past six,' he said. 'You're a bit late, aren't you?'

'I know. It's those dreadful trains. Aunt Maude sent you her love as usual. I'm dying for a drink, aren't you?'

The husband folded his newspaper into a neat rectangle and placed it on the arm of his chair. Then he stood up and crossed over to the sideboard. His wife remained in the centre of the room pulling off her gloves, watching him carefully, wondering how long she ought to wait. He had his back to her now, bending forward to measure the gin, putting his face right up close to the measurer and peering into it as though it were a patient's mouth.

It was funny how small he always looked after the Colonel. The Colonel was huge and bristly, and when you were near to him he smelled faintly of horseradish. This one was small and neat and bony and he didn't really smell of anything at all, except peppermint drops, which he sucked to keep his breath nice for the patients.

'See what I've bought for measuring the vermouth,' he said, holding up a calibrated glass beaker. 'I can get it to the nearest milligram with this.'

'Darling, how clever.'

I really must try to make him change the way he dresses, she told herself. His suits are just too ridiculous for words. There had been a time when she thought they were wonderful, those Edwardian jackets with high lapels and six buttons down the front, but now they merely seemed absurd. So did the narrow stovepipe trousers. You had to have a special sort of face to wear things like that, and Cyril just didn't have it. His was a long bony countenance with a narrow nose and a slightly prognathous jaw, and when you saw it coming up out of the top of one of those tightly fitting old-fashioned suits it looked like a caricature of Sam Weller. He probably thought it looked like Beau Brummell. It was a fact that in the office he invariably greeted female patients with his white coat unbuttoned so that they would catch a glimpse of the trappings underneath; and in some obscure way this was obviously meant to convey the impression that he was a bit of a dog. But Mrs Bixby knew better. The plumage was a bluff. It meant nothing. It reminded her of an ageing peacock strutting on the lawn with only half its feathers left. Or one of those fatuous self-fertilizing flowers – like the dandelion. A dandelion never has to get fertilized for the setting of its seed, and all those brilliant yellow petals are just a waste of time, a boast, a masquerade. What's that word the biologists use? Subsexual. A dandelion is subsexual. So, for that matter, are the summer broods of water fleas. It sounds a bit like Lewis Carroll, she thought – water fleas and dandelions and dentists.

'Thank you, darling,' she said, taking the martini and seating herself on the sofa with her handbag on her lap. 'And what did *you* do last night?'

'I stayed on in the office and cast a few inlays. I also got my accounts up to date.'

'Now really, Cyril, I think it's high time you let other people do your donkey work for you. You're much too important for that sort of thing. Why don't you give the inlays to the mechanic?'

'I prefer to do them myself. I'm extremely proud of my inlays.'

'I know you are, darling, and I think they're absolutely wonderful. They're the best inlays in the whole world. But I don't want you to burn yourself out. And why doesn't that Pulteney woman do the accounts? That's part of her job, isn't it?'

'She does do them. But I have to price everything up first. She doesn't know who's rich and who isn't.'

'This martini is perfect,' Mrs Bixby said, setting down her glass on the side table. 'Quite perfect.' She opened her bag and took out a handkerchief as if to blow her nose.

'Oh look!' she cried, seeing the ticket. 'I forgot to show you this! I found it just now on the seat of my taxi. It's got a number on it, and I thought it might be a lottery ticket or something, so I kept it.'

She handed the small piece of stiff brown paper to her husband, who took it in his fingers and began examining it minutely from all angles, as though it were a suspect tooth.

'You know what this is?' he said slowly.

'No dear, I don't.'

'It's a pawn ticket.'

'A what?'

'A ticket from a pawnbroker. Here's the name and address of the shop – somewhere on Sixth Avenue.'

'Oh dear, I *am* disappointed. I was hoping it might be a ticket for the Irish Sweep.'

'There's no reason to be disappointed,' Cyril Bixby said. 'As a matter of fact this could be rather amusing.'

'Why could it be amusing, darling?'

He began explaining to her exactly how a pawn ticket worked, with particular reference to the fact that anyone possessing the ticket was entitled to claim the article. She listened patiently until he had finished his lecture.

'You think it's worth claiming?' she asked.

'I think it's worth finding out what it is. You see this figure of fifty dollars that's written here? You know what that means?'

'No, dear, what does it mean?'

'It means that the item in question is almost certain to be something quite valuable.'

'You mean it'll be worth fifty dollars?'

'More like five hundred.'

'Five hundred!'

'Don't you understand?' he said. 'A pawnbroker never gives you more than about a tenth of the real value.'

'Good gracious! I never knew that.'

'There's a lot of things you don't know, my dear. Now you listen to me. Seeing that there's no name and address of the owner . . .'

'But surely there's something to say who it belongs to?'

'Not a thing. People often do that. They don't want anyone to know they've been to a pawnbroker. They're ashamed of it.'

'Then you think we can keep it?'

'Of course we can keep it. This is now *our* ticket.'

'You mean *my* ticket,' Mrs Bixby said firmly. 'I found it.'

'My dear girl, what *does* it matter? The important thing is that we are now in a position to go and redeem it any time we like for only fifty dollars. How about that?'

'Oh, what fun!' she cried. 'I think it's terribly exciting, especially when we don't even know what it is. It could be *anything*, isn't that right, Cyril? Absolutely anything!'

'It could indeed, although it's most likely to be either a ring or a watch.'

'But wouldn't it be marvellous if it was a *real* treasure? I mean something *really* old, like a wonderful old vase or a Roman statue.'

'There's no knowing what it might be, my dear. We shall just have to wait and see.'

'I think it's absolutely fascinating! Give me the ticket

and I'll rush over first thing Monday morning and find out!'

'I think I'd better do that.'

'Oh no!' she cried. 'Let *me* do it!'

'I think not. I'll pick it up on my way to work.'

'But it's *my* ticket! *Please* let me do it, Cyril! Why should *you* have all the fun?'

'You don't know these pawnbrokers, my dear. You're liable to get cheated.'

'I wouldn't get cheated, honestly I wouldn't. Give it to me, please.'

'Also you have to have fifty dollars,' he said, smiling. 'You have to pay out fifty dollars in cash before they'll give it to you.'

'I've got that,' she said. 'I think.'

'I'd rather you didn't handle it, if you don't mind.'

'But Cyril, *I found* it. It's mine. Whatever it is, it's mine, isn't that right?'

'Of course it's yours, my dear. There's no need to get so worked up about it.'

'I'm not. I'm just excited, that's all.'

'I suppose it hasn't occurred to you that this might be something entirely masculine – a pocket-watch, for example, or a set of shirt-studs. It isn't only women that go to pawnbrokers, you know.'

'In that case I'll give it to you for Christmas,' Mrs Bixby said magnanimously. 'I'll be delighted. But if it's a woman's thing, I want it myself. Is that agreed?'

'That sounds very fair. Why don't you come with me when I collect it?'

Mrs Bixby was about to say yes to this, but caught herself just in time. She had no wish to be greeted like an old customer by the pawnbroker in her husband's presence.

'No,' she said slowly. 'I don't think I will. You see, it'll be even more thrilling if I stay behind and wait. Oh, I do hope it isn't going to be something that neither of us wants.'

'You've got a point there,' he said. 'If I don't think it's worth fifty dollars, I won't even take it.'

'But you said it would be worth five hundred.'

'I'm quite sure it will. Don't worry.'

'Oh, Cyril, I can hardly wait! Isn't it exciting?'

'It's amusing,' he said, slipping the ticket into his waistcoat pocket. 'There's no doubt about that.'

Monday morning came at last, and after breakfast Mrs Bixby followed her husband to the door and helped him on with his coat.

'Don't work too hard, darling,' she said.

'No, all right.'

'Home at six?'

'I hope so.'

'Are you going to have time to go to that pawnbroker?' she asked.

'My God, I forgot all about it. I'll take a cab and go there now. It's on my way.'

'You haven't lost the ticket, have you?'

'I hope not,' he said, feeling in his waistcoat pocket. 'No, here it is.'

'And you have enough money?'

'Just about.'

'Darling,' she said, standing close to him and straightening his tie, which was perfectly straight. 'If it happens to be something nice, something you think I might like, will you telephone me as soon as you get to the office?'

'If you want me to, yes.'

'You know, I'm sort of hoping it'll be something for you, Cyril. I'd much rather it was for you than for me.'

'That's very generous of you, my dear. Now I must run.'

About an hour later, when the telephone rang, Mrs Bixby was across the room so fast she had the receiver off the hook before the first ring had finished.

'I got it!' he said.

'You did! Oh, Cyril, what was it? Was it something good?'

'Good!' he cried. 'It's fantastic! You wait till you get your eyes on this! You'll swoon!'

'Darling, what is it? Tell me quick!'

'You're a lucky girl, that's what you are.'

'It's for me, then?'

'Of course it's for you. Though how in the world it ever got to be pawned for only fifty dollars I'll be damned if I know. Someone's crazy.'

'Cyril! Stop keeping me in suspense! I can't bear it!'

'You'll go mad when you see it.'

'What is it?'

'Try to guess.'

Mrs Bixby paused. Be careful, she told herself. Be very careful now.

'A necklace,' she said.

'Wrong.'

'A diamond ring.'

'You're not even warm. I'll give you a hint. It's something you can wear.'

'Something I can wear? You mean like a hat?'

'No, it's not a hat,' he said, laughing.

'For goodness' sake, Cyril! Why don't you tell me?'

'Because I want it to be a surprise. I'll bring it home with me this evening.'

'You'll do nothing of the sort!' she cried. 'I'm coming right down there to get it now!'

'I'd rather you didn't do that.'

'Don't be so silly, darling. Why shouldn't I come?'

'Because I'm too busy. You'll disorganize my whole morning schedule. I'm half an hour behind already.'

'Then I'll come in the lunch hour. All right?'

'I'm not having a lunch hour. Oh well, come at one thirty then, while I'm having a sandwich. Good-bye.'

At half past one precisely, Mrs Bixby arrived at Dr Bixby's place of business and rang the bell. Her husband, in his white dentist's coat, opened the door himself.

'Oh, Cyril, I'm so excited!'

'So you should be. You're a lucky girl, did you know that?' He led her down the passage and into the surgery.

'Go and have your lunch, Miss Pulteney,' he said to the assistant, who was busy putting instruments into the sterilizer. 'You can finish that when you come back.' He waited until the girl had gone, then he walked over to a closet that he used for hanging up his clothes and stood in front of it, pointing with his finger. 'It's in there,' he said. 'Now – shut your eyes.'

Mrs Bixby did as she was told. Then she took a deep breath and held it, and in the silence that followed she could hear him opening the cupboard door and there was a soft swishing sound as he pulled out a garment from among the other things hanging there.

'All right! You can look!'

'I don't dare to,' she said, laughing.

'Go on. Take a peek.'

Coyly, beginning to giggle, she raised one eyelid a fraction of an inch, just enough to give her a dark blurry view of the man standing there in his white overalls holding something up in the air.

'Mink!' he cried. 'Real mink!'

At the sound of the magic word she opened her eyes quick, and at the same time she actually started forward in order to clasp the coat in her arms.

But there was no coat. There was only a ridiculous little fur neckpiece dangling from her husband's hand.

'Feast your eyes on that!' he said, waving it in front of her face.

Mrs Bixby put a hand up to her mouth and started backing away. I'm going to scream, she told herself. I just know it. I'm going to scream.

'What's the matter, my dear? Don't you like it?' He stopped waving the fur and stood staring at her, waiting for her to say something.

'Why yes,' she stammered. 'I . . . I . . . think it's . . . it's lovely . . . really lovely.'

'Quite took your breath away for a moment there, didn't it?'

'Yes, it did.'

'Magnificent quality,' he said. 'Fine colour, too. You know something, my dear? I reckon a piece like this would cost you two or three hundred dollars at least if you had to buy it in a shop.'

'I don't doubt it.'

There were two skins, two narrow mangy-looking skins with their heads still on them and glass beads in their eye sockets and little paws hanging down. One of them had the rear end of the other in its mouth, biting it.

'Here,' he said. 'Try it on.' He leaned forward and draped the thing round her neck, then stepped back to admire. 'It's perfect. It really suits you. It isn't everyone who has mink, my dear.'

'No, it isn't.'

'Better leave it behind when you go shopping or they'll all think we're millionaires and start charging us double.'

'I'll try to remember that, Cyril.'

'I'm afraid you mustn't expect anything else for Christmas. Fifty dollars was rather more than I was going to spend anyway.'

He turned away and went over to the basin and began washing his hands. 'Run along now, my dear, and buy yourself a nice lunch. I'd take you out myself but I've got old man Gorman in the waiting-room with a broken clasp on his denture.'

Mrs Bixby moved towards the door.

I'm going to kill that pawnbroker, she told herself. I'm going right back there to the shop this very minute and I'm going to throw this filthy neckpiece right in his face and if he refuses to give me back my coat I'm going to kill him.

'Did I tell you I was going to be late home tonight?' Cyril Bixby said, still washing his hands.

'No.'

'It'll probably be at least eight thirty the way things look at the moment. It may even be nine.'

'Yes, all right. Good-bye.' Mrs Bixby went out, slamming the door behind her.

At that precise moment, Miss Pulteney, the secretary-assistant, came sailing past her down the corridor on her way to lunch.

'Isn't it a gorgeous day?' Miss Pulteney said as she went by, flashing a smile. There was a lilt in her walk, a little whiff of perfume attending her, and she looked like a queen, just exactly like a queen in the beautiful black mink coat that the Colonel had given to Mrs Bixby.

Claud's Dog

First published in *Someone Like You* (1953)

Rummins

The sun was up over the hills now and the mist had cleared and it was wonderful to be striding along the road with the dog in the early morning, especially when it was autumn, with the leaves changing to gold and yellow and sometimes one of them breaking away and falling slowly, turning slowly over in the air, dropping noiselessly right in front of him on to the grass beside the road. There was a small wind up above, and he could hear the beeches rustling and murmuring like a crowd of people.

This was always the best time of the day for Claud Cubbage. He gazed approvingly at the rippling velvety hindquarters of the greyhound trotting in front of him.

'Jackie,' he called softly. 'Hey, Jackson. How you feeling, boy?'

The dog half turned at the sound of its name and gave a quick acknowledging wag of the tail.

There would never be another dog like this Jackie, he told himself. How beautiful the slim streamlining, the small pointed head, the yellow eyes, the black mobile nose. Beautiful the long neck, the way the deep brisket curved back and up out of sight into no stomach at all. See how he walked upon his toes, noiselessly, hardly touching the surface of the road at all.

'Jackson,' he said. 'Good old Jackson.'

In the distance, Claud could see Rummins' farmhouse, small, narrow and ancient, standing back behind the hedge on the right-hand side.

I'll turn round there, he decided. That'll be enough for today.

Rummins, carrying a pail of milk across the yard, saw him coming down the road. He set the pail down slowly and came forward to the gate, leaning both arms on the topmost bar, waiting.

'Morning, Mr Rummins,' Claud said. It was necessary to be polite to Rummins because of eggs.

Rummins nodded and leaned over the gate, looking critically at the dog.

'Looks well,' he said.

'He is well.'

'When's he running?'

'I don't know, Mr Rummins.'

'Come on. When's he running?'

'He's only ten months yet, Mr Rummins. He's not even schooled properly, honest.'

The small beady eyes of Rummins peered suspiciously over the top of the gate. 'I wouldn't mind betting a couple of quid you're having it off with him somewhere secret soon.'

Claud moved his feet uncomfortably on the black road surface. He disliked very much this man with the wide frog mouth, the broken teeth, the shifty eyes; and most of all he disliked having to be polite to him because of eggs.

'That hayrick of yours opposite,' he said, searching desperately for another subject. 'It's full of rats.'

'All hayricks got rats.'

'Not like this one. Matter of fact we've been having a touch of trouble with the authorities about that.'

Rummins glanced up sharply. He didn't like trouble with the authorities. Any man who sells eggs blackmarket and kills pigs without a permit is wise to avoid contact with that sort of people.

'What kind of trouble?'

'They sent the ratcatcher along.'

'You mean just for a few rats?'

'A few! Blimey, it's *swarming*!'

'Never.'

'Honest it is, Mr Rummins. There's hundreds of 'em.'

'Didn't the ratcatcher catch 'em?'

'No.'

'Why?'

'I reckon they're too artful.'

Rummins began thoughtfully to explore the inner rim of one nostril with the end of his thumb, holding the nose-flap between thumb and finger as he did so.

'I wouldn't give thank you for no ratcatchers,' he said. 'Ratcatchers is government men working for the soddin' government and I wouldn't give thank you for 'em.'

'Nor me, Mr Rummins. All ratcatchers is slimy cunning creatures.'

'Well,' Rummins said, sliding fingers under his cap to scratch the head, 'I was coming over soon anyway to fetch in that rick. Reckon I might just as well do it today as any other time. I don't want no government men nosing around my stuff, thank you very much.'

'Exactly, Mr Rummins.'

'We'll be over later – Bert and me.' With that he turned and ambled off across the yard.

Around three in the afternoon, Rummins and Bert were seen riding slowly up the road in a cart drawn by a ponderous and magnificent black carthorse. Opposite the filling-station the cart turned off into the field and stopped near the hayrick.

'This ought to be worth seeing,' I said. 'Get the gun.'

Claud fetched the rifle and slipped a cartridge into the breech.

I strolled across the road and leaned against the open gate. Rummins was on the top of the rick now and cutting away at the cord that bound the thatching. Bert remained in the cart, fingering the four-foot-long knife.

Bert had something wrong with one eye. It was pale grey all over, like a boiled fish-eye, and although it was motionless in its socket it appeared always to be looking at you and following you round, the way the eyes of the people in some of those portraits do, in the museums. Wherever you stood and wherever Bert was looking, there was this faulty eye fixing you sideways with a cold stare, boiled and misty pale with a little black dot in the centre, like a fish-eye on a plate.

In his build he was the opposite of his father, who was

short and squat like a frog. Bert was a tall, reedy, boneless boy, loose at the joints, even the head loose upon the shoulders, falling sideways as though perhaps it was too heavy for the neck.

'You only made this rick last June,' I said to him. 'Why take it away so soon?'

'Dad wants it.'

'Funny time to cut a new rick, November.'

'Dad wants it,' Bert repeated, and both his eyes, the sound one and the other, stared down at me with a look of absolute vacuity.

'Going to all that trouble stacking it and thatching it and then pulling it down five months later.'

'Dad wants it.' Bert's nose was running and he kept wiping it with the back of his hand and wiping the back of the hand on his trousers.

'Come on, Bert,' Rummins called, and the boy climbed up on to the rick and stood in the place where the thatch had been removed. He took the knife and began to cut down into the tight-packed hay with an easy-swinging, sawing movement, holding the handle with both hands and rocking his body like a man sawing wood with a big saw. I could hear the crisp cutting noise of the blade against the dry hay and the noise becoming softer as the knife sank deeper into the rick.

'Claud's going to take a pot at the rats as they come out.'

The man and the boy stopped abruptly and looked across the road at Claud, who was leaning against the red pump with rifle in hand.

'Tell him to put that bloody rifle away,' Rummins said.

'He's a good shot. He won't hit you.'

'No one's potting no rats alongside of me, don't matter how good they are.'

'You'll insult him.'

'Tell him to put it away,' Rummins said, slow and hostile. 'I don't mind dogs nor sticks but I'll be buggered if I'll have rifles.'

The two on the hayrick watched while Claud did as he was told, then they resumed their work in silence. Soon Bert came down into the cart, and reaching out with both hands he pulled a slice of solid hay away from the rick so that it dropped neatly into the cart beside him.

A rat, grey-black, with a long tail, came out of the base of the rick and ran into the hedge.

'A rat,' I said.

'Kill it,' Rummins said. 'Why don't you get a stick and kill it?'

The alarm had been given now and the rats were coming out quicker, one or two of them every minute, fat and long-bodied, crouching close to the ground as they ran through the grass into the hedge. Whenever the horse saw one of them it twitched its ears and followed it with uneasy rolling eyes.

Bert had climbed back on top of the rick and was cutting out another bale. Watching him, I saw him suddenly stop, hesitate for perhaps a second, then again begin to cut, but very cautiously this time, and now I could hear a different sound, a muffled rasping noise as the blade of the knife grated against something hard.

Bert pulled out the knife and examined the blade, testing it with his thumb. He put it back, letting it down gingerly into the cut, feeling gently downward until it came again upon the hard object; and once more, when he made another cautious little sawing movement, there came that grating sound.

Rummins turned his head and looked over his shoulder at the boy. He was in the act of lifting an armful of loosened thatch, bending forward with both hands grasping the straw, but he stopped dead in the middle of what he was doing and looked at Bert. Bert remained still, hands holding the handle of the knife, a look of bewilderment on his face. Behind, the sky was a pale clear blue and the two figures up there on the hayrick stood out sharp and black like an etching against the paleness.

Then Rummins' voice, louder than usual, edged with an unmistakable apprehension that the loudness did nothing to conceal: 'Some of them haymakers is too bloody careless what they put on a rick these days.'

He paused, and again the silence, the men motionless, and across the road Claud leaning motionless against the red pump. It was so quiet suddenly we could hear a woman's voice far down the valley on the next farm calling the men to food.

Then Rummins again, shouting where there was no need to shout: 'Go on, then! Go on an' cut through it, Bert! A little stick of wood won't hurt the soddin' knife!'

For some reason, as though perhaps scenting trouble, Claud came strolling across the road and joined me leaning on the gate. He didn't say anything, but both of us seemed to know that there was something disturbing about these two men, about the stillness that surrounded them and especially about Rummins himself. Rummins was frightened. Bert was frightened too. And now as I watched them, I became conscious of a small vague image moving just below the surface of my memory. I tried desperately to reach back and grasp it. Once I almost touched it, but it slipped away and when I went after it I found myself travelling back and back through many weeks, back into the yellow days of summer – the warm wind blowing down the valley from the south, the big beech trees heavy with their foliage, the fields turning to gold, the harvesting, the haymaking, the rick – the building of the rick.

Instantly I felt a fine electricity of fear running over the skin of my stomach.

Yes – the building of the rick. When was it we had built it? June? That was it, of course – a hot muggy day in June with the clouds low overhead and the air thick with the smell of thunder.

And Rummins had said, 'Let's for God's sake get it in quick before the rain comes.'

And Ole Jimmy had said, 'There ain't going to be no rain. And there ain't no hurry either. You know very well when thunder's in the south it don't cross over into the valley.'

Rummins, standing up in the cart handing out the pitchforks, had not answered him. He was in a furious brooding temper because of his anxiety about getting in the hay before it rained.

'There ain't gin' to be no rain before evening.' Ole Jimmy had repeated, looking at Rummins; and Rummins had stared back at him, the eyes glimmering with a slow anger.

All through the morning we had worked without a pause, loading the hay into the cart, trundling it across the field, pitching it out on to the slowly growing rick that stood over by the gate opposite the filling-station. We could hear the thunder in the south as it came towards us and moved away again. Then it seemed to return and remain stationary somewhere beyond the hills, rumbling intermittently. When we looked up we could see the clouds overhead moving and changing shape in the turbulence of the upper air, but on the ground it was hot and muggy and there was no breath of wind. We worked slowly, listlessly, in the heat, shirts wet with sweat, faces shining.

Claud and I had worked beside Rummins on the rick itself, helping to shape it, and I could remember how very hot it had been and the flies around my face and the sweat pouring out everywhere; and especially I could remember the grim scowling presence of Rummins beside me, working with a desperate urgency and watching the sky and shouting at the men to hurry.

At noon, in spite of Rummins, we had knocked off for lunch.

Claud and I had sat down under the hedge with Ole Jimmy and another man called Wilson who was a soldier home on leave, and it was too hot to do much talking. Wilson had some bread and cheese and a canteen of cold tea. Ole Jimmy had a satchel that was an old gas-mask container, and in this, closely packed, standing upright with their necks protruding, were six pint bottles of beer.

'Come on,' he said, offering a bottle to each of us.

'I'd like to buy one from you,' Claud said, knowing very well the old man had little money.

'Take it.'

'I must pay you.'

'Don't be so daft. Drink it.'

He was a very good old man, good and clean, with a clean pink face that he shaved each day. He had used to be a carpenter, but they retired him at the age of seventy and that was some years before. Then the Village Council, seeing him still active, had given him the job of looking after the newly built children's playground, of maintaining the swings and see-saws in good repair and also of acting as a kind of gentle watchdog, seeing that none of the kids hurt themselves or did anything foolish.

That was a fine job for an old man to have and everybody seemed pleased with the way things were going – until a certain Saturday night. That night Ole Jimmy had got drunk and gone reeling and singing down the middle of the High Street with such a howling noise that people got out of their beds to see what was going on below. The next morning they had sacked him, saying he was a waster and a drunkard not fit to associate with young children in the playground.

But then an astonishing thing happened. The first day that he stayed away – a Monday it was – not one single child came near the playground.

Nor the next day, nor the one after that.

All week the swings and the see-saws and the high slide with steps going up to it stood deserted. Not a child went near them. Instead they followed Ole Jimmy out into a field behind the rectory and played their games there with him watching; and the result of all this was that after a while the Council had had no alternative but to give the old man back his job.

He still had it now and he still got drunk and no one said anything about it any more. He left it only for a few days each year, at haymaking time. All his life Ole Jimmy had loved to go haymaking and he wasn't going to give it up yet.

'You want one?' he asked now, holding a bottle out to Wilson, the soldier.

'No thanks. I got tea.'

'They say tea's good on a hot day.'

'It is. Beer makes me sleepy.'

'If you like,' I said to Ole Jimmy, 'we could walk across to the filling-station and I'll do you a couple of nice sandwiches? Would you like that?'

'Beer's plenty. There's more food in one bottle of beer, me lad, than twenty sandwiches.'

He smiled at me, showing two rows of pale-pink, toothless gums, but it was a pleasant smile and there was nothing repulsive about the way the gums showed.

We sat for a while in silence. The soldier finished his bread and cheese and lay back on the ground, tilting his hat forward over his face. Ole Jimmy had drunk three bottles of beer, and now he offered the last to Claud and me.

'No thanks.'

'No thanks. One's plenty for me.'

The old man shrugged, unscrewed the stopper, tilted

his head back and drank, pouring the beer into his mouth with the lips held open so the liquid ran smoothly without gurgling down his throat. He wore a hat that was of no colour at all and of no shape, and it did not fall off when he tilted back his head.

'Ain't Rummins goin' to give that old horse a drink?' he asked, lowering the bottle, looking across the field at the great carthorse that stood steaming between the shafts of the cart.

'Not Rummins.'

'Horses is thirsty, just the same as us.' Ole Jimmy paused, still looking at the horse. 'You got a bucket of water in that place of yours there?'

'Of course.'

'No reason why we shouldn't give the old horse a drink then, is there?'

'That's a very good idea. We'll give him a drink.'

Claud and I both stood up and began walking towards the gate, and I remember turning and calling to the old man: 'You quite sure you wouldn't like me to bring you a nice sandwich? Won't take a second to make.'

He shook his head and waved the bottle at us and said something about taking himself a little nap. We went on through the gate over the road to the filling-station.

I suppose we stayed away for about an hour attending to customers and getting ourselves something to eat, and when at length we returned, Claud carrying the bucket of water, I noticed that the rick was at least six foot high.

'Some water for the old horse,' Claud said, looking hard

at Rummins, who was up in the cart pitching hay on to the rick.

The horse put its head in the bucket, sucking and blowing gratefully at the water.

'Where's Ole Jimmy?' I asked. We wanted the old man to see the water, because it had been his idea.

When I asked the question there was a moment, a brief moment, when Rummins hesitated, pitchfork in mid-air, looking around him.

'I brought him a sandwich,' I added.

'Bloody old fool drunk too much beer and gone off home to sleep,' Rummins said.

I strolled along the hedge back to the place where we had been sitting with Ole Jimmy. The five empty bottles were lying there in the grass. So was the satchel. I picked up the satchel and carried it back to Rummins.

'I don't think Ole Jimmy's gone home, Mr Rummins,' I said, holding up the satchel by the long shoulder-band. Rummins glanced at it but made no reply. He was in a frenzy of haste now because the thunder was closer, the clouds blacker, the heat more oppressive than ever.

Carrying the satchel, I started back to the filling-station, where I remained for the rest of the afternoon, serving customers. Towards evening, when the rain came, I glanced across the road and noticed that they had got the hay in and were laying a tarpaulin over the rick.

In a few days the thatcher arrived and took the tarpaulin off and made a roof of straw instead. He was a good thatcher and he made a fine roof with long straw, thick and well-packed. The slope was nicely angled, the edges cleanly clipped, and it was a pleasure to look at it from the road or from the door of the filling-station.

All this came flooding back to me now as clearly as if it were yesterday – the building of the rick on that hot thundery day in June, the yellow field, the sweet woody smell of the hay; and Wilson the soldier, with tennis shoes on his feet, Bert with the boiled eye, Ole Jimmy with the clean old face, the pink naked gums; and Rummins, the broad dwarf, standing up in the cart scowling at the sky because he was anxious about the rain.

At this very moment, there he was again, this Rummins, crouching on top of the rick with a sheaf of thatch in his arms, looking round at the son, the tall Bert, motionless also, both of them black like silhouettes against the sky, and once again I felt the fine electricity of fear as it came and went in little waves over the skin of my stomach.

'Go on and cut through it, Bert,' Rummins said, speaking loudly.

Bert put pressure on the big knife and there was a high grating noise as the edge of the blade sawed across something hard. It was clear from Bert's face that he did not like what he was doing.

It took several minutes before the knife was through – then again at last the softer sound of the blade slicing the tight-packed hay and Bert's face turned sideways to the father, grinning with relief, nodding inanely.

'Go on and cut it out,' Rummins said, and still he did not move.

Bert made a second vertical cut the same depth as the

first; then he got down and pulled the bale of hay so it came away cleanly from the rest of the rick like a chunk of cake, dropping into the cart at his feet.

Instantly the boy seemed to freeze, staring stupidly at the newly exposed face of the rick, unable to believe or perhaps refusing to believe what this thing was that he had cut in two.

Rummins, who knew very well what it was, had turned away and was climbing quickly down the other side of the rick. He moved so fast he was through the gate and half-way across the road before Bert started to scream.

Claud's Dog

First published in *Someone Like You* (1953)

Mr Hoddy

They got out of the car and went in the front door of Mr Hoddy's house.

'I've an idea Dad's going to question you rather sharp tonight,' Clarice whispered.

'About what, Clarice?'

'The usual stuff. Jobs and things like that. And whether you can support me in a fitting way.'

'Jackie's going to do that,' Claud said. 'When Jackie wins there won't be any need for any jobs . . .'

'Don't you ever mention Jackie to my dad, Claud Cubbage, or that'll be the end of it. If there's one thing in the world he can't abide it's greyhounds. Don't you ever forget that.'

'Oh Christ,' Claud said.

'Tell him something else – anything – anything to make him happy, see?' And with that she led Claud into the parlour.

Mr Hoddy was a widower, a man with a prim sour mouth and an expression of eternal disapproval all over his face. He had the small, close-together teeth of his daughter Clarice, the same suspicious, inward look about the eyes, but none of her freshness and vitality, none of her warmth. He was a small sour apple of a man, grey-skinned and shrivelled, with a dozen or so surviving strands of black hair pasted across the dome of his bald head. But a very superior man was Mr Hoddy, a grocer's assistant, one who wore a spotless white gown at his work, who handled large quantities of such precious commodities as butter and sugar, who was deferred to, even smiled at, by every housewife in the village.

Claud Cubbage was never quite at his ease in this house and that was precisely as Mr Hoddy intended it. They were sitting round the fire in the parlour with cups of tea in their hands, Mr Hoddy in the best chair to the right of the fireplace, Claud and Clarice on the sofa, decorously separated by a wide space. The younger daughter, Ada, was on a hard upright chair to the left, and they made a little circle round the fire, a stiff, tense little circle, primly tea-sipping.

'Yes, Mr Hoddy,' Claud was saying, 'you can be quite sure both Gordon and me's got quite a number of nice little ideas up our sleeves this very moment. It's only a question of taking our time and making sure which is going to be the most profitable.'

'What sort of ideas?' Mr Hoddy asked, fixing Claud with his small, disapproving eyes.

'Ah, there you are now. That's it, you see.' Claud shifted uncomfortably on the sofa. His blue lounge suit was tight around his chest, and it was especially tight between his legs, up in the crutch. The tightness in his crutch was actually painful to him and he wanted terribly to hitch it downward.

'This man you call Gordon, I thought he had a profitable

business out there as it is,' Mr Hoddy said. 'Why does he want to change?'

'Absolutely right, Mr Hoddy. It's a first-rate business. But it's a good thing to keep expanding, see. New ideas is what we're after. Something I can come in on as well and take a share of the profits.'

'Such as what?'

Mr Hoddy was eating a slice of currant cake, nibbling it round the edges, and his small mouth was like the mouth of a caterpillar biting a tiny curved slice out of the edge of a leaf.

'Such as what?' he asked again.

'There's long conferences, Mr Hoddy, takes place every day between Gordon and me about these different matters of business.'

'Such as what?' he repeated, relentless.

Clarice glanced sideways at Claud, encouraging. Claud turned his large slow eyes upon Mr Hoddy, and he was silent. He wished Mr Hoddy wouldn't push him around like this, always shooting questions at him and glaring at him and acting just exactly like he was the bloody adjutant or something.

'Such as what?' Mr Hoddy said, and this time Claud knew that he was not going to let go. Also, his instinct warned him that the old man was trying to create a crisis.

'Well now,' he said, breathing deep. 'I don't really want to go into details until we got it properly worked out. All we're doing so far is turning our ideas over in our minds, see.'

'All I'm asking,' Mr Hoddy said irritably, 'is what *sort* of business are you contemplating? I presume that it's respectable?'

'Now *please*, Mr Hoddy. You don't for one moment think we'd even so much as *consider* anything that wasn't absolutely and entirely respectable, do you?'

Mr Hoddy grunted, stirring his tea slowly, watching Claud. Clarice sat mute and fearful on the sofa, gazing into the fire.

'I've never been in favour of starting a business,' Mr Hoddy pronounced, defending his own failure in that line. 'A good respectable job is all a man should wish for. A respectable job in respectable surroundings. Too much hokey-pokey in business for my liking.'

'The thing is this,' Claud said, desperate now. 'All I want is to provide my wife with everything she can possibly desire. A house to live in and furniture and a flower garden and a washing-machine and all the best things in the world. That's what I want to do, and you can't do that on an ordinary wage, now can you? It's impossible to get enough money to do that unless you go into business, Mr Hoddy. You'll surely agree with me there?'

Mr Hoddy, who had worked for an ordinary wage all his life, didn't much like this point of view.

'And don't you think *I* provide everything my family wants, might I ask?'

'Oh yes, and more!' Claud cried fervently. 'But *you've* got a very superior job, Mr Hoddy, and that makes all the difference.'

'But what *sort* of business are you thinking of?' the man persisted.

Claud sipped his tea to give himself a little more time and he couldn't help wondering how the miserable old bastard's face would look if he simply up and told him the truth right there and then, if he'd said, What we've got, Mr Hoddy, if you really wants to know, is a couple of greyhounds and one's a perfect ringer for the other and we're going to bring off the biggest goddam gamble in the history of flapping, see. He'd like to watch the old bastard's face if he said that, he really would.

They were all waiting for him to proceed now, sitting there with cups of tea in their hands staring at him and waiting for him to say something good. 'Well,' he said, speaking very slowly because he was thinking deep. 'I've been pondering something a long time now, something as'll make more money even than Gordon's second-hand cars or anything else come to that, and practically no expense involved.' That's better, he told himself. Keep going along like that.

'And what might that be?'

'Something so queer, Mr Hoddy, there isn't one in a million would even believe it.'

'Well, what is it?' Mr Hoddy placed his cup carefully on the little table beside him and leaned forward to listen. And Claud, watching him, knew more than ever that this man and all those like him were his enemies. It was the Mr Hoddys were the trouble. They were all the same. He knew them all, with their clean ugly hands, their grey skin, their acrid mouths, their tendency to develop little round bulging bellies just below the waistcoat; and always the unctuous curl of the nose, the weak chin, the suspicious eyes that were dark and moved too quick. The Mr Hoddys. Oh Christ.

'Well, what is it?'

'It's an absolute gold-mine, Mr Hoddy, honestly it is.'

'I'll believe that when I hear it.'

'It's a thing so simple and amazing most people wouldn't even bother to do it.' He had it now – something he *had* actually been thinking seriously about for a long time, something he'd always wanted to do. He leaned across and put his teacup carefully on the table beside Mr Hoddy's, then, not knowing what to do with his hands, placed them on his knees, palms downward.

'Well, come on man, what is it?'

'It's maggots,' Claud answered softly.

Mr Hoddy jerked back as though someone had squirted water in his face. 'Maggots!' he said, aghast. '*Maggots?* What on earth do you mean, maggots?' Claud had forgotten that this word was almost unmentionable in any self-respecting grocer's shop. Ada began to giggle, but Clarice glanced at her so malignantly the giggle died on her mouth.

'That's where the money is, starting a maggot factory.'

'Are you trying to be funny?'

'Honestly, Mr Hoddy, it may sound a bit queer, and that's simply because you never heard it before, but it's a little gold-mine.'

'A *maggot factory*! Really now, Cubbage! Please be sensible.'

Clarice wished her father wouldn't call him Cubbage.

'You never heard speak of a maggot factory, Mr Hoddy?'

'I certainly have not!'

'There's maggot factories going now, real big companies with managers and directors and all, and you know what, Mr Hoddy? They're making millions!'

'Nonsense, man.'

'And you know why they're making millions?' Claud paused, but he did not notice now that his listener's face was slowly turning yellow. 'It's because of the enormous demand for maggots, Mr Hoddy.'

At that moment Mr Hoddy was listening also to other voices, the voices of his customers across the counter – Mrs Rabbits, for instance, as he sliced off her ration of butter, Mrs Rabbits with her brown moustache and always talking so loud and saying, Well, well, well; he could hear her now saying, Well, well, well Mr Hoddy, so your Clarice got married last week, did she? Very nice too, I must say, and what was it you said her husband does, Mr Hoddy?'

He owns a maggot factory, Mrs Rabbits.

No thank you, he told himself, watching Claud with his small, hostile eyes. No thank you very much indeed. I don't want that.

'I can't say,' he announced primly, 'that I myself have ever had occasion to purchase a maggot.'

'Now you come to mention it, Mr Hoddy, nor have I. Nor has many other people we know. But let me ask you something else. How many times you had occasion to purchase . . . a crown wheel and pinion, for instance?'

This was a shrewd question and Claud permitted himself a slow mawkish smile.

'What's that got to do with maggots?'

'Exactly this – that certain people buy certain things, see. You never bought a crown wheel and pinion in your life, but that don't say there isn't men getting rich this very moment making them – because there is. It's the same with maggots!'

'Would you mind telling me who these unpleasant people are who buy maggots?'

'Maggots are bought by fishermen, Mr Hoddy. Amateur fishermen. There's thousands and thousands of fishermen all over the country going out every week-end fishing the rivers and all of them wanting maggots. Willing to pay good money for them, too. You go along the river there anywhere you like above Marlow on a Sunday and you'll see them *lining* the banks. Sitting there one beside the other simply *lining* the banks on both sides.'

'Those men don't buy maggots. They go down the bottom of the garden and dig worms.'

'Now that's just where you're wrong, Mr Hoddy, if you'll allow me to say so. That's just where you're absolutely wrong. They want maggots, not worms.'

'In that case they get their own maggots.'

'They don't *want* to get their own maggots. Just imagine Mr Hoddy, it's Saturday afternoon and you're going out fishing and a nice clean tin of maggots arrives by post and all you've got to do is slip it in the fishing bag and away you go. You don't think fellers is going out digging for worms and hunting for maggots when they can have them delivered right to their very doorsteps like that just for a bob or two, do you?'

'And might I ask how you propose to run this maggot

factory of yours?' When he spoke the word 'maggot', it seemed as if he were spitting out a sour little pip from his mouth.

'Easiest thing in the world to run a maggot factory.' Claud was gaining confidence now and warming to his subject. 'All you need is a couple of old oil drums and a few lumps of rotten meat or a sheep's head, and you put them in the oil drums and that's all you do. The flies do the rest.'

Had he been watching Mr Hoddy's face he would probably have stopped there.

'Of course, it's not quite as easy as it sounds. What you've got to do next is feed up your maggots with special diet. Bran and milk. And then when they get big and fat you put them in pint tins and post them off to your customers. Five shillings a pint they fetch. *Five shillings a pint!*' he cried, slapping the knee. 'You just imagine that, Mr Hoddy! And they say one bluebottle'll lay twenty pints easy!'

He paused again, but merely to marshal his thoughts, for there was no stopping him now.

'And there's another thing, Mr Hoddy. A good maggot factory don't just breed ordinary maggots, you know. Every fisherman's got his own tastes. Maggots are commonest, but also there's lug worms. Some fishermen won't have nothing but lug worms. And of course there's coloured maggots. Ordinary maggots are white, but you get them all sorts of different colours by feeding them special foods, see. Red ones and green ones and black ones and you can even get blue ones if you know what to feed them. The most difficult thing of all in a maggot factory is a blue maggot, Mr Hoddy.'

Claud stopped to catch his breath. He was having a vision now – the same vision that accompanied all his dreams of wealth – of an immense factory building with tall chimneys and hundreds of happy workers streaming in through the wide wrought-iron gates and Claud himself sitting in his luxurious office directing operations with a calm and splendid assurance.

'There's people with brains studying these things this very minute,' he went on. 'So you got to jump in quick unless you want to get left out in the cold. That's the secret of big business, jumping in quick before all the others, Mr Hoddy.'

Clarice, Ada and the father sat absolutely still looking straight ahead. None of them moved or spoke. Only Claud rushed on.

'Just so long as you make sure your maggots is alive when you post 'em. They've got to be wiggling, see. Maggots is no good unless they're wiggling. And when we really get going, when we've built up a little capital, then we'll put up some glasshouses.'

Another pause, and Claud stroked his chin. 'Now I expect you're all wondering why a person should want glasshouses in a maggot factory. Well – I'll tell you. It's for the flies in the winter, see. Most important to take care of your flies in the winter.'

'I think that's enough, thank you, Cubbage,' Mr Hoddy said suddenly.

Claud looked up and for the first time he saw the expression on the man's face. It stopped him cold.

'I don't want to hear any more about it,' Mr Hoddy said.

'All I'm trying to do, Mr Hoddy,' Claud cried, 'is give your little girl everything she can possibly desire. That's all I'm thinking of night and day, Mr Hoddy.'

'Then all I hope is you'll be able to do it without the help of maggots.'

'Dad!' Clarice cried, alarmed. 'I simply won't have you talking to Claud like that.'

'I'll talk to him how I wish, thank you, Miss.'

'I think it's time I was getting along,' Claud said. 'Good night.'

The Hitch-hiker

First published in *Atlantic Monthly*
(August 1977)

I had a new car. It was an exciting toy, a big BMW 3.3 Li, which means 3.3 litre, long wheelbase, fuel injection. It had a top speed of 129 mph and terrific acceleration. The body was pale blue. The seats inside were darker blue and they were made of leather, genuine soft leather of the finest quality. The windows were electrically operated and so was the sun-roof. The radio aerial popped up when I switched on the radio, and disappeared when I switched it off. The powerful engine growled and grunted impatiently at slow speeds, but at sixty miles an hour the growling stopped and the motor began to purr with pleasure.

I was driving up to London by myself. It was a lovely June day. They were haymaking in the fields and there were buttercups along both sides of the road. I was whispering along at seventy miles an hour, leaning back comfortably in my seat, with no more than a couple of fingers resting lightly on the wheel to keep her steady. Ahead of me I saw a man thumbing a lift. I touched the footbrake and brought the car to a stop beside him. I always stopped for hitch-hikers. I knew just how it used to feel to be standing on the side of a country road watching the cars go by. I hated the drivers for pretending they didn't see me, especially the ones in big cars with three empty seats. The large expensive cars seldom stopped. It was always the smaller ones that offered you a lift, or the old rusty ones, or the ones that were already crammed full of children and the driver would say, 'I think we can squeeze in one more.'

The hitch-hiker poked his head through the open window and said, 'Going to London, guv'nor?'

'Yes,' I said, 'jump in.'

He got in and I drove on.

He was a small ratty-faced man with grey teeth. His eyes were dark and quick and clever, like a rat's eyes, and his ears were slightly pointed at the top. He had a cloth cap on his head and he was wearing a greyish-coloured jacket with enormous pockets. The grey jacket, together with the quick eyes and the pointed ears, made him look more than anything like some sort of a huge human rat.

'What part of London are you headed for?' I asked him.

'I'm goin' right through London and out the other side,' he said. 'I'm goin' to Epsom, for the races. It's Derby Day today.'

'So it is,' I said. 'I wish I were going with you. I love betting on horses.'

'I never bet on horses,' he said. 'I don't even watch 'em run. That's a stupid silly business.'

'Then why do you go?' I asked.

He didn't seem to like that question. His little ratty face went absolutely blank and he sat there staring straight ahead at the road, saying nothing.

'I expect you help to work the betting machines or something like that,' I said.

'That's even sillier,' he answered. 'There's no fun working them lousy machines and selling tickets to mugs. Any fool could do that.'

There was a long silence. I decided not to question him any more. I remembered how irritated I used to get in my hitch-hiking days when drivers kept asking *me* questions. Where are you going? Why are you going there? What's your job? Are you married? Do you have a girl-friend? What's her name? How old are you? And so on and so forth. I used to hate it.

'I'm sorry,' I said. 'It's none of my business what you do. The trouble is, I'm a writer, and most writers are terrible nosey parkers.'

'You write books?' he asked.

'Yes.'

'Writin' books is OK,' he said. 'It's what I call a skilled trade. I'm in a skilled trade too. The folks I despise is them that spend all their lives doin' crummy old routine jobs with no skill in 'em at all. You see what I mean?'

'Yes.'

'The secret of life,' he said, 'is to become very very good at somethin' that's very very 'ard to do.'

'Like you,' I said.

'Exactly. You and me both.'

'What makes you think that *I'm* any good at my job?' I asked. 'There's an awful lot of bad writers around.'

'You wouldn't be drivin' about in a car like this if you weren't no good at it,' he answered. 'It must've cost a tidy packet, this little job.'

'It wasn't cheap.'

'What can she do flat out?' he asked.

'One hundred and twenty-nine miles an hour,' I told him.

'I'll bet she won't do it.'

'I'll bet she will.'

'All car makers is liars,' he said. 'You can buy any car you like and it'll never do what the makers say it will in the ads.'

'This one will.'

'Open 'er up then and prove it,' he said. 'Go on, guv'nor, open 'er right up and let's see what she'll do.'

There is a roundabout at Chalfont St Peter and immediately beyond it there's a long straight section of dual carriageway. We came out of the roundabout on to the carriageway and I pressed my foot down on the accelerator. The big car leaped forwards as though she'd been stung. In ten seconds or so, we were doing ninety.

'Lovely!' he cried. 'Beautiful! Keep goin'!'

I had the accelerator jammed right down against the floor and I held it there.

'One hundred!' he shouted ... 'A hundred and five! ... A hundred and ten! ... A hundred and fifteen! Go on! Don't slack off!'

I was in the outside lane and we flashed past several cars as though they were standing still – a green Mini, a big cream-coloured Citroën, a white Land Rover, a huge truck with a container on the back, an orange-coloured Volkswagen Minibus ...

'A hundred and twenty!' my passenger shouted, jumping up and down. 'Go on! Go on! Get 'er up to one-two-nine!'

At that moment, I heard the scream of a police siren. It

was so loud it seemed to be right inside the car, and then a policeman on a motor-cycle loomed up alongside us on the inside lane and went past us and raised a hand for us to stop.

'Oh, my sainted aunt!' I said. 'That's torn it!'

The policeman must have been doing about a hundred and thirty when he passed us, and he took plenty of time slowing down. Finally, he pulled into the side of the road and I pulled in behind him. 'I didn't know police motor-cycles could go as fast as that,' I said rather lamely.

'That one can,' my passenger said. 'It's the same make as yours. It's a BMW R90S. Fastest bike on the road. That's what they're usin' nowadays.'

The policeman got off his motor-cycle and leaned the machine sideways on to its prop stand. Then he took off his gloves and placed them carefully on the seat. He was in no hurry now. He had us where he wanted us and he knew it.

'This is real trouble,' I said. 'I don't like it one bit.'

'Don't talk to 'im any more than is necessary, you understand,' my companion said. 'Just sit tight and keep mum.'

Like an executioner approaching his victim, the policeman came strolling slowly towards us. He was a big meaty man with a belly, and his blue breeches were skintight around his enormous thighs. His goggles were pulled up on the helmet, showing a smouldering red face with wide cheeks.

We sat there like guilty schoolboys, waiting for him to arrive.

'Watch out for this man,' my passenger whispered. ''Ee looks mean as the devil.'

The policeman came round to my open window and placed one meaty hand on the sill. 'What's the hurry?' he said.

'No hurry, officer,' I answered.

'Perhaps there's a woman in the back having a baby and you're rushing her to hospital? Is that it?'

'No, officer.'

'Or perhaps your house is on fire and you're dashing home to rescue the family from upstairs?' His voice was dangerously soft and mocking.

'My house isn't on fire, officer.'

'In that case,' he said, 'you've got yourself into a nasty mess, haven't you? Do you know what the speed limit is in this country?'

'Seventy,' I said.

'And do you mind telling me exactly what speed you were doing just now?'

I shrugged and didn't say anything.

When he spoke next, he raised his voice so loud that I jumped. '*One hundred and twenty miles per hour!*' he barked. 'That's *fifty* miles an hour over the limit!'

He turned his head and spat out a big gob of spit. It landed on the wing of my car and started sliding down over my beautiful blue paint. Then he turned back again and stared hard at my passenger. 'And who are you?' he asked sharply.

'He's a hitch-hiker,' I said. 'I'm giving him a lift.'

'I didn't ask you,' he said. 'I asked him.'

''Ave I done somethin' wrong?' my passenger asked. His voice was as soft and oily as haircream.

'That's more than likely,' the policeman answered. 'Anyway, you're a witness. I'll deal with you in a minute. Driving-licence,' he snapped, holding out his hand.

I gave him my driving-licence.

He unbuttoned the left-hand breast-pocket of his tunic and brought out the dreaded book of tickets. Carefully, he copied the name and address from my licence. Then he gave it back to me. He strolled round to the front of the car and read the number from the number-plate and wrote that down as well. He filled in the date, the time and the details of my offence. Then he tore out the top copy of the ticket. But before handing it to me, he checked that all the information had come through clearly on his own carbon copy. Finally, he replaced the book in his tunic pocket and fastened the button.

'Now you,' he said to my passenger, and he walked around to the other side of the car. From the other breast-pocket he produced a small black notebook. 'Name?' he snapped.

'Michael Fish,' my passenger said.

'Address?'

'Fourteen, Windsor Lane, Luton.'

'Show me something to prove this is your real name and address,' the policeman said.

My passenger fished in his pockets and came out with a driving-licence of his own. The policeman checked the name and address and handed it back to him. 'What's your job?' he asked sharply.

'I'm an 'od carrier.'

'A *what*?'

'An 'od carrier.'

'Spell it.'

'H-O-D C-A- . . .'

'That'll do. And what's a hod carrier, may I ask?'

'An 'od carrier, officer, is a person 'oo carries the cement up the ladder to the bricklayer. And the 'od is what 'ee carries it in. It's got a long 'andle, and on the top you've got two bits of wood set at an angle . . .'

'All right, all right. Who's your employer?'

'Don't 'ave one. I'm unemployed.'

The policeman wrote all this down in the black notebook. Then he returned the book to its pocket and did up the button.

'When I get back to the station I'm going to do a little checking up on you,' he said to my passenger.

'Me? What've I done wrong?' the rat-faced man asked.

'I don't like your face, that's all,' the policeman said. 'And we just might have a picture of it somewhere in our files.' He strolled round the car and returned to my window.

'I suppose you know you're in serious trouble,' he said to me.

'Yes, officer.'

'You won't be driving this fancy car of yours again for a very long time, not after *we've* finished with you. You won't be driving *any* car again come to that for several years. And a good thing, too. I hope they lock you up for a spell into the bargain.'

'You mean prison?' I asked, alarmed.

'Absolutely,' he said, smacking his lips. 'In the clink. Behind the bars. Along with all the other criminals who break the law. *And* a hefty fine into the bargain. Nobody will be more pleased about that than me. I'll see you in court, both of you. You'll be getting a summons to appear.'

He turned away and walked over to his motor-cycle. He flipped the prop stand back into position with his foot and swung his leg over the saddle. Then he kicked the starter and roared off up the road out of sight.

'Phew!' I gasped. 'That's done it.'

'We was caught,' my passenger said. 'We was caught good and proper.'

'I was caught, you mean.'

'That's right,' he said. 'What you goin' to do now, guv'nor?'

'I'm going straight up to London to talk to my solicitor,' I said. I started the car and drove on.

'You mustn't believe what 'ee said to you about goin' to prison,' my passenger said. 'They don't put nobody in the clink just for speedin'.'

'Are you sure of that?' I asked.

'I'm positive,' he answered. 'They can take your licence away and they can give you a whoppin' big fine, but that'll be the end of it.'

I felt tremendously relieved.

'By the way,' I said, 'why did you lie to him?'

'Who, me?' he said. 'What makes you think I lied?'

'You told him you were an unemployed hod carrier. But you told *me* you were in a highly skilled trade.'

'So I am,' he said. 'But it don't pay to tell everythin' to a copper.'

'So what *do* you do?' I asked him.

'Ah,' he said slyly. 'That'd be tellin', wouldn't it?'

'Is it something you're ashamed of?'

'Ashamed?' he cried. 'Me, ashamed of my job? I'm about as proud of it as anybody could be in the entire world!'

'Then why won't you tell me?'

'You writers really is nosey parkers, aren't you?' he said. 'And you ain't goin' to be 'appy, I don't think, until you've found out exactly what the answer is?'

'I don't really care one way or the other,' I told him, lying.

He gave me a crafty little ratty look out of the sides of his eyes. 'I think you do care,' he said. 'I can see it in your face that you think I'm in some kind of a very peculiar trade and you're just achin' to know what it is.'

I didn't like the way he read my thoughts. I kept quiet and stared at the road ahead.

'You'd be right, too,' he went on. 'I *am* in a very peculiar trade. I'm in the queerest peculiar trade of 'em all.'

I waited for him to go on.

'That's why I 'as to be extra careful 'oo I'm talkin' to, you see. 'Ow am I to know, for instance, you're not another copper in plain clothes?'

'Do I look like a copper?'

'No,' he said. 'You don't. And you ain't. Any fool could tell that.'

He took from his pocket a tin of tobacco and a packet of cigarette papers and started to roll a cigarette. I was watching him out of the corner of one eye, and the speed with which he performed this rather difficult operation was incredible. The cigarette was rolled and ready in about five seconds. He ran his tongue along the edge of the paper, stuck it down and popped the cigarette between his lips. Then, as if from nowhere, a lighter appeared in his hand. The lighter flamed. The cigarette was lit. The lighter disappeared. It was altogether a remarkable performance.

'I've never seen anyone roll a cigarette as fast as that,' I said.

'Ah,' he said, taking a deep suck of smoke. 'So you noticed.'

'Of course I noticed. It was quite fantastic.'

He sat back and smiled. It pleased him very much that I had noticed how quickly he could roll a cigarette. 'You want to know what makes me able to do it?' he asked.

'Go on then.'

'It's because I've got fantastic fingers. These fingers of mine,' he said, holding up both hands high in front of him, 'are quicker and cleverer than the fingers of the best piano player in the world!'

'Are you a piano player?'

'Don't be daft,' he said. 'Do I look like a piano player?'

I glanced at his fingers. They were so beautifully shaped, so slim and long and elegant, they didn't seem to belong to the rest of him at all. They looked more like the fingers of a brain surgeon or a watchmaker.

'My job,' he went on, 'is a hundred times more difficult than playin' the piano. Any twerp can learn to do that. There's titchy little kids learnin' to play the piano in almost any 'ouse you go into these days. That's right, ain't it?'

'More or less,' I said.

'Of course it's right. But there's not one person in ten million can learn to do what I do. Not one in ten million! 'Ow about that?'

'Amazing,' I said.

'You're darn right it's amazin',' he said.

'I think I know what you do,' I said. 'You do conjuring tricks. You're a conjurer.'

'Me?' he snorted. 'A conjurer? Can you picture me goin' round crummy kids' parties makin' rabbits come out of top 'ats?'

'Then you're a card player. You get people into card games and deal yourself marvellous hands.'

'Me! A rotten card-sharper!' he cried. 'That's a miserable racket if ever there was one.'

'All right. I give up.'

I was taking the car along slowly now, at no more than forty miles an hour, to make quite sure I wasn't stopped again. We had come on to the main London–Oxford road and were running down the hill towards Denham.

Suddenly, my passenger was holding up a black leather belt in his hand. 'Ever seen this before?' he asked. The belt had a brass buckle of unusual design.

'Hey!' I said. 'That's mine, isn't it? It *is* mine! Where did you get it?'

He grinned and waved the belt gently from side to side.

'Where d'you think I got it?' he said. 'Off the top of your trousers, of course.'

I reached down and felt for my belt. It was gone.

'You mean you took it off me while we've been driving along?' I asked, flabbergasted.

He nodded, watching me all the time with those little black ratty eyes.

'That's impossible,' I said. 'You'd have to undo the buckle and slide the whole thing out through the loops all the way round. I'd have seen you doing it. And even if I hadn't seen you, I'd have felt it.'

'Ah, but you didn't, did you?' he said, triumphant. He dropped the belt on his lap, and now all at once there was a brown shoelace dangling from his fingers. 'And what about this, then?' he exclaimed, waving the shoelace.

'What about it?' I said.

'Anyone round 'ere missin' a shoelace?' he asked, grinning.

I glanced down at my shoes. The lace of one of them was missing. 'Good grief!' I said. 'How did you do that? I never saw you bending down.'

'You never saw nothin',' he said proudly. 'You never even saw me move an inch. And you know why?'

'Yes,' I said. 'Because you've got fantastic fingers.'

'Exactly right!' he cried. 'You catch on pretty quick, don't you?' He sat back and sucked away at his home-made cigarette, blowing the smoke out in a thin stream against the windshield. He knew he had impressed me greatly with those two tricks, and this made him very happy. 'I don't want to be late,' he said. 'What time is it?'

'There's a clock in front of you,' I told him.

'I don't trust car clocks,' he said. 'What does your watch say?'

I hitched up my sleeve to look at the watch on my wrist. It wasn't there. I looked at the man. He looked back at me, grinning.

'You've taken that, too,' I said.

He held out his hand and there was my watch lying in his palm. 'Nice bit of stuff, this,' he said. 'Superior quality. Eighteen-carat gold. Easy to flog, too. It's never any trouble gettin' rid of quality goods.'

'I'd like it back, if you don't mind,' I said rather huffily.

He placed the watch carefully on the leather tray in front of him. 'I wouldn't nick anything from you, guv'nor,' he said. 'You're my pal. You're giving me a lift.'

'I'm glad to hear it,' I said.

'All I'm doin' is answerin' your questions,' he went on. 'You asked me what I did for a livin' and I'm showin' you.'

'What else have you got of mine?'

He smiled again, and now he started to take from the pocket of his jacket one thing after another that belonged to me – my driving-licence, a key-ring with four keys on it, some pound notes, a few coins, a letter from my publishers, my diary, a stubby old pencil, a cigarette-lighter, and last of all, a beautiful old sapphire ring with pearls around it belonging to my wife. I was taking the ring up to the jeweller in London because one of the pearls was missing.

'Now *there's* another lovely piece of goods,' he said, turning the ring over in his fingers. 'That's eighteenth century, if I'm not mistaken, from the reign of King George the Third.'

'You're right,' I said, impressed. 'You're absolutely right.'

He put the ring on the leather tray with the other items.

'So you're a pickpocket,' I said.

'I don't like that word,' he answered. 'It's a coarse and vulgar word. Pickpockets is coarse and vulgar people who only do easy little amateur jobs. They lift money from blind old ladies.'

'What do you call yourself, then?'

'Me? I'm a fingersmith. I'm a professional fingersmith.' He spoke the words solemnly and proudly, as though he were telling me he was the President of the Royal College of Surgeons or the Archbishop of Canterbury.

'I've never heard that word before,' I said. 'Did you invent it?'

'Of course I didn't invent it,' he replied. 'It's the name given to them who's risen to the very top of the profession. You've 'eard of a goldsmith and a silversmith, for instance. They're experts with gold and silver. I'm an expert with my fingers, so I'm a fingersmith.'

'It must be an interesting job.'

'It's a marvellous job,' he answered. 'It's lovely.'

'And that's why you go to the races?'

'Race meetings is easy meat,' he said. 'You just stand around after the race, watchin' for the lucky ones to queue up and draw their money. And when you see someone collectin' a big bundle of notes, you simply follows after 'im and 'elps yourself. But don't get me wrong, guv'nor. I never takes nothin' from a loser. Nor from poor people neither. I only go after them as can afford it, the winners and the rich.'

'That's very thoughtful of you,' I said. 'How often do you get caught?'

'Caught?' he cried, disgusted. '*Me* get caught! It's only pickpockets get caught. Fingersmiths never. Listen, I could take the false teeth out of your mouth if I wanted to and you wouldn't even catch me!'

'I don't have false teeth,' I said.

'I know you don't,' he answered. 'Otherwise I'd 'ave 'ad 'em out long ago!'

I believed him. Those long slim fingers of his seemed able to do anything.

We drove on for a while without talking.

'That policeman's going to check up on you pretty thoroughly,' I said. 'Doesn't that worry you a bit?'

'Nobody's checkin' up on me,' he said.

'Of course they are. He's got your name and address written down most carefully in his black book.'

The man gave me another of his sly, ratty little smiles. 'Ah,' he said. 'So 'ee 'as. But I'll bet 'ee ain't got it all written down in 'is memory as well. I've never known a copper yet with a decent memory. Some of 'em can't even remember their own names.'

'What's memory got to do with it?' I asked. 'It's written down in his book, isn't it?'

'Yes, guv'nor, it is. But the trouble is, 'ee's lost the book. 'Ee's lost both books, the one with my name in it *and* the one with yours.'

In the long delicate fingers of his right hand, the man

was holding up in triumph the two books he had taken from the policeman's pockets. 'Easiest job I ever done,' he announced proudly.

I nearly swerved the car into a milk-truck, I was so excited.

'That copper's got nothin' on either of us now,' he said.

'You're a genius!' I cried.

''Ee's got no names, no addresses, no car number, no nothin',' he said.

'You're brilliant!'

'I think you'd better pull in off this main road as soon as possible,' he said. 'Then we'd better build a little bonfire and burn these books.'

'You're a fantastic fellow,' I exclaimed.

'Thank you, guv'nor,' he said. 'It's always nice to be appreciated.'

The Surgeon

First published in *Playboy*, January 1988

'You have done extraordinarily well,' Robert Sandy said, seating himself behind the desk. 'It's altogether a splendid recovery. I don't think there's any need for you to come and see me any more.'

The patient finished putting on his clothes and said to the surgeon, 'May I speak to you, please, for another moment?'

'Of course you may,' Robert Sandy said. 'Take a seat.'

The man sat down opposite the surgeon and leaned forward, placing his hands, palms downward, on the top of the desk. 'I suppose you still refuse to take a fee?' he said.

'I've never taken one yet and I don't propose to change my ways at this time of life,' Robert Sandy told him pleasantly. 'I work entirely for the National Health Service and they pay me a very fair salary.'

Robert Sandy MA, M.CHIR, FRCS, had been at The Radcliffe Infirmary in Oxford for eighteen years and he was now fifty-two years old, with a wife and three grown-up children. Unlike many of his colleagues, he did not hanker after fame and riches. He was basically a simple man utterly devoted to his profession.

It was now seven weeks since his patient, a university undergraduate, had been rushed into Casualty by ambulance after a nasty car accident in the Banbury Road not far from the hospital. He was suffering from massive abdominal injuries and he had lost consciousness. When the call came through from Casualty for an emergency surgeon, Robert Sandy was up in his office having a cup of tea after a fairly arduous morning's work which had included a gall-bladder, a prostate and a total colostomy, but for some reason he happened to be the only general surgeon available at that moment. He took one more sip of his tea, then walked straight back into the operating theatre and started scrubbing up all over again.

After three and a half hours on the operating table, the patient was still alive and Robert Sandy had done everything he could to save his life. The next day, to the surgeon's considerable surprise, the man was showing signs that he was going to survive. In addition, his mind was lucid and he was speaking coherently. It was only then, on the morning after the operation, that Robert Sandy began to realize that he had an important person on his hands. Three dignified gentlemen from the Saudi Arabian Embassy, including the Ambassador himself, came into the hospital and the first thing they wanted was to call in all manner of celebrated surgeons from Harley Street to advise on the case. The patient, with bottles suspended all round his bed and tubes running into many parts of his body, shook his head and murmured something in Arabic to the Ambassador.

'He says he wants only you to look after him,' the Ambassador said to Robert Sandy.

'You are very welcome to call in anyone else you choose for consultation,' Robert Sandy said.

'Not if he doesn't want us to,' the Ambassador said. 'He says you have saved his life and he has absolute faith in you. We must respect his wishes.'

The Ambassador then told Robert Sandy that his patient was none other than a prince of royal blood. In other words, he was one of the many sons of the present King of Saudi Arabia.

A few days later, when the Prince was off the danger list, the Embassy tried once again to persuade him to make a change. They wanted him to be moved to a far more luxurious hospital that catered only for private patients, but the Prince would have none of it. 'I stay here,' he said, 'with the surgeon who saved my life.'

Robert Sandy was touched by the confidence his patient was putting in him, and throughout the long weeks of recovery, he did his best to ensure that this confidence was not misplaced.

And now, in the consulting-room, the Prince was saying, 'I do wish you would allow me to pay you for all you have done, Mr Sandy.' The young man had spent three years at Oxford and he knew very well that in England a surgeon was always addressed as 'Mister' and not 'Doctor'. 'Please let me pay you, Mr Sandy,' he said.

Robert Sandy shook his head. 'I'm sorry,' he answered, 'but I still have to say no. It's just a personal rule of mine and I won't break it.'

'But dash it all, you saved my life,' the Prince said, tapping the palms of his hands on the desk.

'I did no more than any other competent surgeon would have done,' Robert Sandy said.

The Prince took his hands off the desk and clasped them on his lap. 'All right, Mr Sandy, even though you refuse a fee, there is surely no reason why my father should not give you a small present to show his gratitude.'

Robert Sandy shrugged his shoulders. Grateful patients quite often gave him a case of whisky or a dozen bottles of wine and he accepted these things gracefully. He never expected them, but he was awfully pleased when they arrived. It was a nice way of saying thank you.

The Prince took from his jacket pocket a small pouch made of black velvet and he pushed it across the desk. 'My father,' he said, 'has asked me to tell you how enormously indebted he is to you for what you have done. He told me that whether you took a fee or not, I was to make sure you accepted this little gift.'

Robert Sandy looked suspiciously at the black pouch, but he made no move to take it.

'My father,' the Prince went on, 'said also to tell you that in his eyes my life is without price and that nothing on earth can repay you adequately for having saved it. This is simply a . . . what shall we call it . . . a present for your next birthday. A small birthday present.'

'He shouldn't give me anything,' Robert Sandy said.

'Look at it, please,' the Prince said.

Rather gingerly, the surgeon picked up the pouch and loosened the silk thread at the opening. When he tipped it upside down, there was a flash of brilliant light as something ice-white dropped on to the plain wooden desk-top. The stone was about the size of a cashew nut or a bit larger, perhaps three-quarters of an inch long from end to end, and it was pear-shaped, with a very sharp point at the narrow end. Its many facets glimmered and sparkled in the most wonderful way.

'Good gracious me,' Robert Sandy said, looking at it but not yet touching it. 'What is it?'

'It's a diamond,' the Prince said. 'Pure white. It's not especially large, but the colour is good.'

'I really can't accept a present like this,' Robert Sandy said. 'No, it wouldn't be right. It must be quite valuable.'

The Prince smiled at him. 'I must tell you something, Mr Sandy,' he said. 'Nobody refuses a gift from the King. It would be a terrible insult. It has never been done.'

Robert Sandy looked back at the Prince. 'Oh dear,' he said. 'You *are* making it awkward for me, aren't you?'

'It is not awkward at all,' the Prince said. 'Just take it.'

'You could give it to the hospital.'

'We have already made a donation to the hospital,' the Prince said. 'Please take it, not just for my father, but for me as well.'

'You are very kind,' Robert Sandy said. 'All right, then. But I feel quite embarrassed.' He picked up the diamond and placed it in the palm of one hand. 'There's never been a diamond in our family before,' he said. 'Gosh, it is beautiful, isn't it. You must please convey my thanks to His Majesty and tell him I shall always treasure it.'

'You don't actually have to hang on to it,' the Prince said. 'My father would not be in the least offended if you were to sell it. Who knows, one day you might need a little pocket-money.'

'I don't think I shall sell it,' Robert Sandy said. 'It is too lovely. Perhaps I shall have it made into a pendant for my wife.'

'What a nice idea,' the Prince said, getting up from his chair. 'And please remember what I told you before. You and your wife are invited to my country at any time. My father would be happy to welcome you both.'

'That's very good of him,' Robert Sandy said. 'I won't forget.'

When the Prince had gone, Robert Sandy picked up the diamond again and examined it with total fascination. It was dazzling in its beauty, and as he moved it gently from side to side in his palm, one facet after the other caught the light from the window and flashed brilliantly with blue and pink and gold. He glanced at his watch. It was ten minutes past three. An idea had come to him. He picked up the telephone and asked his secretary if there was anything else urgent for him to do that afternoon. If there wasn't, he told her, then he thought he might leave early.

'There's nothing that can't wait until Monday,' the secretary said, sensing that for once this most hard-working of men had some special reason for wanting to go.

'I've got a few things of my own I'd very much like to do.'

'Off you go, Mr Sandy,' she said. 'Try to get some rest over the weekend. I'll see you on Monday.'

In the hospital car park, Robert Sandy unchained his bicycle, mounted and rode out on to the Woodstock Road. He still bicycled to work every day unless the weather was foul. It kept him in shape and it also meant his wife could have the car. There was nothing odd about that. Half the population of Oxford rode on bicycles. He turned into the Woodstock Road and headed for The High. The only good jeweller in town had his shop in The High, halfway up on the right, and he was called H. F. Gold. It said so above the window, and most people knew that H stood for Harry. Harry Gold had been there a long time, but Robert had only been inside once, years ago, to buy a small bracelet for his daughter as a confirmation present.

He parked his bike against the kerb outside the shop and went in. A woman behind the counter asked if she could help him.

'Is Mr Gold in?' Robert Sandy said.

'Yes, he is.'

'I would like to see him privately for a few minutes, if I may. My name is Sandy.'

'Just a minute, please.' The woman disappeared through a door at the back, but in thirty seconds she returned and said, 'Will you come this way, please.'

Robert Sandy walked into a large untidy office in which a small, oldish man was seated behind a partners' desk. He wore a grey goatee beard and steel spectacles, and he stood up as Robert approached him.

'Mr Gold, my name is Robert Sandy. I am a surgeon at The Radcliffe. I wonder if you can help me.'

'I'll do my best, Mr Sandy. Please sit down.'

'Well, it's an odd story,' Robert Sandy said. 'I recently operated on one of the Saudi princes. He's in his third year at Magdalen and he'd been involved in a nasty car accident. And now he has given me, or rather his father has given me, a fairly wonderful-looking diamond.'

'Good gracious me,' Mr Gold said. 'How very exciting.'

'I didn't want to accept it, but I'm afraid it was more or less forced on me.'

'And you would like me to look at it?'

'Yes, I would. You see, I haven't the faintest idea whether it's worth five hundred pounds or five thousand, and it's only sensible that I should know roughly what the value is.'

'Of course you should,' Harry Gold said. 'I'll be glad to help you. Doctors at the Radcliffe have helped *me* a great deal over the years.'

Robert Sandy took the black pouch out of his pocket and placed it on the desk. Harry Gold opened the pouch and tipped the diamond into his hand. As the stone fell into his palm, there was a moment when the old man appeared to freeze. His whole body became motionless as he sat there staring at the brilliant shining thing that lay before him. Slowly, he stood up. He walked over to the window and held the stone so that daylight fell upon it. He turned it over with one finger. He didn't say a word. His expression never changed. Still holding the diamond, he returned to his desk and from a drawer he took out a single sheet of clean white paper. He made a loose fold in the paper and placed the diamond in the fold. Then he returned to the window and stood there for a full minute studying the diamond that lay in the fold of paper.

'I am looking at the colour,' he said at last. 'That's the first thing to do. One always does that against a fold of white paper and preferably in a north light.'

'Is that a north light?'

'Yes, it is. This stone is a wonderful colour, Mr Sandy.

As fine a D colour as I've ever seen. In the trade, the very best quality white is called a D colour. In some places it's called a River. That's mostly in Scandinavia. A layman would call it a Blue White.'

'It doesn't look very blue to me,' Robert Sandy said.

'The purest whites always contain a trace of blue,' Harry Gold said. 'That's why in the old days they always put a blue-bag into the washing water. It made the clothes whiter.'

'Ah yes, of course.'

Harry Gold went back to his desk and took out from another drawer a sort of hooded magnifying glass. 'This is a ten-times loupe,' he said, holding it up.

'What did you call it?'

'A loupe. It is simply a jeweller's magnifier. With this, I can examine the stone for imperfections.'

Back once again at the window, Harry Gold began a minute examination of the diamond through the ten-times loupe, holding the paper with the stone on it in one hand and the loupe in the other. This process took maybe four minutes. Robert Sandy watched him and kept quiet.

'So far as I can see,' Harry Gold said, 'it is completely flawless. It really is a most lovely stone. The quality is superb and the cutting is very fine, though definitely not modern.'

'Approximately how many facets would there be on a diamond like that?' Robert Sandy asked.

'Fifty-eight.'

'You mean you know exactly?'

'Yes, I know exactly.'

'Good Lord. And what roughly would you say it is worth?'

'A diamond like this,' Harry Gold said, taking it from the paper and placing it in his palm, 'a D colour stone of this size and clarity would command on inquiry a trade price of between twenty-five and thirty thousand dollars a carat. In the shops it would cost you double that. Up to sixty thousand dollars a carat in the retail market.'

'Great Scott!' Robert Sandy cried, jumping up. The little jeweller's words seemed to have lifted him clean out of his seat. He stood there, stunned.

'And now,' Harry Gold was saying, 'we must find out precisely how many carats it weighs.' He crossed over to a shelf on which there stood a small metal apparatus. 'This is simply an electronic scale,' he said. He slid back a glass door and placed the diamond inside. He twiddled a couple of knobs, then he read off the figures on a dial. 'It weighs fifteen point two seven carats,' he said. 'And that, in case it interests you, makes it worth about half a million dollars in the trade and over one million dollars if you bought it in a shop.'

'You are making me nervous,' Robert Sandy said, laughing nervously.

'If I owned it,' Harry Gold said, 'it would make *me* nervous. Sit down again, Mr Sandy, so you don't faint.'

Robert Sandy sat down.

Harry Gold took his time settling himself into his chair behind the big partner's desk. 'This is quite an occasion, Mr Sandy,' he said. 'I don't often have the pleasure of giving someone quite such a startlingly wonderful shock as this. I think I'm enjoying it more than you are.'

'I am too shocked to be really enjoying it yet,' Robert Sandy said. 'Give me a moment or two to recover.'

'Mind you,' Harry Gold said, 'one wouldn't expect much less from the King of the Saudis. Did you save the young prince's life?'

'I suppose I did, yes.'

'Then that explains it.' Harry Gold had put the diamond back on to the fold of white paper on his desk, and he sat there looking at it with the eyes of a man who loved what he saw. 'My guess is that this stone came from the treasure-chest of old King Ibn Saud of Arabia. If that is the case, then it will be totally unknown in the trade, which makes it even more desirable. Are you going to sell it?'

'Oh gosh, I don't know what I am going to do with it,' Robert Sandy said. 'It's all so sudden and confusing.'

'May I give you some advice.'

'Please do.'

'If you *are* going to sell it, you should take it to auction. An unseen stone like this would attract a lot of interest, and the wealthy private buyers would be sure to come in and bid against the trade. And if you were able to reveal its provenance as well, telling them that it came directly from the Saudi Royal Family, then the price would go through the roof.'

'You have been more than kind to me,' Robert Sandy said. 'When I do decide to sell it, I shall come first of all to you for advice. But tell me, does a diamond really cost twice as much in the shops as it does in the trade?'

'I shouldn't be telling you this,' Harry Gold said, 'but I'm afraid it does.'

'So if you buy one in Bond Street or anywhere else like that, you are actually paying twice its intrinsic worth?'

'That's more or less right. A lot of young ladies have received nasty shocks when they've tried to re-sell jewellery that has been given to them by gentlemen.'

'So diamonds are not a girl's best friend?'

'They are still very friendly things to have,' Harry Gold said, 'as you have just found out. But they are not generally a good investment for the amateur.'

Outside in The High, Robert Sandy mounted his bicycle and headed for home. He was feeling totally light headed. It was as though he had just finished a whole bottle of good wine all by himself. Here he was, solid old Robert Sandy, sedate and sensible, cycling through the streets of Oxford with more than half a million dollars in the pocket of his old tweed jacket! It was madness. But it was true.

He arrived back at his house in Acacia Road at about half past four and parked his bike in the garage alongside the car. Suddenly he found himself running along the little concrete path that led to the front door. 'Now stop that!' he said aloud, pulling up short. 'Calm down. You've got to make this really good for Betty. Unfold it slowly.' But oh, he simply *could not wait* to give the news to his lovely wife and watch her face as he told her the whole story of his afternoon. He found her in the kitchen packing some jars of home-made jam into a basket.

'Robert!' she cried, delighted as always to see him. 'You're home early! How nice!'

He kissed her and said, 'I *am* a bit early, aren't I?'

'You haven't forgotten we're going to the Renshaws for the week-end? We have to leave fairly soon.'

'I had forgotten,' he said. 'Or maybe I hadn't. Perhaps that's why I'm home early.'

'I thought I'd take Margaret some jam.'

'Good,' he said. 'Very good. You take her some jam. That's a very good idea to take Margaret some jam.'

There was something in the way he was acting that made her swing round and stare at him. 'Robert,' she said, 'what's happened? There's something the matter.'

'Pour us each a drink,' he said. 'I've got a bit of news for you.'

'Oh darling, it's not something awful, is it?'

'No,' he said. 'It's something funny. I think you'll like it.'

'You've been made Head of Surgery!'

'It's funnier than that,' he said. 'Go on, make a good stiff drink for each of us and sit down and I'll tell you.'

'It's a bit early for drinks,' she said, but she got the ice-tray from the fridge and started making his whisky and soda. While she was doing this, she kept glancing up at him nervously. She said, 'I don't think I've ever seen you quite like this before. You are wildly excited about something and you are pretending to be very calm. You're all red in the face. Are you sure it's good news?'

'I *think* it is,' he said, 'but I'll let you judge that for yourself.' He sat down at the kitchen table and watched her as she put the glass of whisky in front of him.

'All right,' she said. 'Come on. Let's have it.'

'Get a drink for yourself first,' he said.

'My goodness, what is this?' she said, but she poured

some gin into a glass and was reaching for the ice-tray when he said, 'More than that. Give yourself a good stiff one.'

'Now I *am* worried,' she said, but she did as she was told and then added ice and filled the glass up with tonic. 'Now then,' she said, sitting down beside him at the table, 'get it off your chest.'

Robert began telling his story. He started with the Prince in the consulting-room and he spun it out long and well so that it took a good ten minutes before he came to the diamond.

'It must be quite a whopper,' she said, 'to make you go all red in the face and funny-looking.'

He reached into his pocket and took out the little black pouch and put it on the table. 'There it is,' he said. 'What do you think?'

She loosened the silk cord and tipped the stone into her hand. 'Oh, my God!' she cried. 'It's absolutely stunning!'

'It is, isn't it.'

'It's amazing.'

'I haven't told you the whole story yet,' he said, and while his wife rolled the diamond from the palm of one hand to the other, he went on to tell her about his visit to Harry Gold in The High. When he came to the point where the jeweller began to talk about value, he stopped and said, 'So what do you think he said it was worth?'

'Something pretty big,' she said. 'It's bound to be. I mean just *look* at it!'

'Go on then, make a guess. How much?'

'Ten thousand pounds,' she said. 'I really don't have any idea.'

'Try again.'

'You mean, it's more?'

'Yes, it's quite a lot more.'

'Twenty thousand pounds!'

'Would you be thrilled if it was worth as much as that?'

'Of course, I would, darling. Is it really worth twenty thousand pounds?'

'Yes,' he said. 'And the rest.'

'Now don't be a beast, Robert. Just tell me what Mr Gold said.'

'Take another drink of gin.'

She did so, then put down the glass, looking at him and waiting.

'It is worth at least half a million dollars and very probably over a million.'

'You're joking!' Her words came out in a kind of gasp.

'It's known as a pear-shape,' he said. 'And where it comes to a point at this end, it's as sharp as a needle.'

'I'm completely stunned,' she said, still gasping.

'You wouldn't have thought half a million, would you?'

'I've never in my life had to think in those sort of figures,' she said. She stood up and went over to him and gave him a huge hug and a kiss. 'You really are the most wonderful and stupendous man in the world!' she cried.

'I was totally bowled over,' he said. 'I still am.'

'Oh Robert!' she cried, gazing at him with eyes bright as two stars. 'Do you realize what this means? It means we can get Diana and her husband out of that horrid little flat and buy them a small house!'

'By golly, you're right!'

'And we can buy a decent flat for John and give him a better allowance all the way through his medical school! And Ben . . . Ben wouldn't have to go on a motor-bike to work all through the freezing winters. We could get him something better. And . . . and . . . and . . .'

'And what?' he asked, smiling at her.

'And you and I can take a really good holiday for once and go wherever we please! We can go to Egypt and Turkey and you can visit Baalbek and all the other places you've been longing to go to for years and years!' She was quite breathless with the vista of small pleasures that were unfolding in her dreams. 'And you can start collecting some really nice pieces for once in your life as well!'

Ever since he had been a student, Robert Sandy's passion had been the history of the Mediterranean countries, Italy, Greece, Turkey, Syria and Egypt, and he had made himself into something of an expert on the ancient world of those various civilizations. He had done it by reading and studying and by visiting, when he had the time, the British Museum and the Ashmolean. But with three children to educate and with a job that paid only a reasonable salary, he had never been able to indulge this passion as he would have liked. He wanted above all to visit some of the grand remote regions of Asia Minor and also the now below-ground village of Babylon in Iraq and he would love to see the Arch of Ctesiphon and the Sphinx at Memphis and a hundred other things and places, but neither the time nor the money had ever been available. Even so, the long coffee-table in the living-room was covered with small objects and fragments that he had managed to pick up cheaply here and there through his life. There was a mysterious pale alabaster ushaptiu in the form of a mummy from Upper Egypt which he knew was Pre-Dynastic from about 700 BC. There was a bronze bowl from Lydia with an engraving on it of a horse, and an early Byzantine twisted silver necklace, and a section of a wooden painted mask from an Egyptian sarcophagus, and a Roman red-ware bowl, and a small black Etruscan dish, and perhaps fifty other fragile and interesting little pieces. None was particularly valuable, but Robert Sandy loved them all.

'Wouldn't that be marvellous?' his wife was saying. 'Where shall we go first?'

'Turkey,' he said.

'Listen,' she said, pointing to the diamond that lay sparkling on the kitchen table, 'you'd better put your fortune away somewhere safe before you lose it.'

'Today is Friday,' he said. 'When do we get back from the Renshaws?'

'Sunday night.'

'And what are we going to do with our million-pound rock in the meanwhile? Take it with us in my pocket?'

'No,' she said, 'that would be silly. You really cannot walk around with a million pounds in your pocket for a whole weekend. It's got to go into a safe-deposit box at the bank. We should do it now.'

'It's Friday night, my darling. All the banks are closed till next Monday.'

'So they are,' she said. 'Well then, we'd better hide it somewhere in the house.'

'The house will be empty till we come back,' he said. 'I don't think that's a very good idea.'

'It's better than carrying it around in your pocket or in my handbag.'

'I'm not leaving it in the house. An empty house is always liable to be burgled.'

'Come on, darling,' she said, 'surely we can think of a place where no one could possibly find it.'

'In the tea-pot,' he said.

'Or bury it in the sugar-basin,' she said.

'Or put it in the bowl of one of my pipes in the pipe-rack,' he said. 'With some tobacco over it.'

'Or under the soil of the azalea plant,' she said.

'Hey, that's not bad, Betty. That's the best so far.'

They sat at the kitchen table with the shining stone lying there between them, wondering very seriously what to do with it for the next two days while they were away.

'I still think it's best if I take it with me,' he said.

'I don't, Robert. You'll be feeling in your pocket every five minutes to make sure it's still there. You won't relax for one moment.'

'I suppose you're right,' he said. 'Very well, then. *Shall* we bury it under the soil of the azalea plant in the sitting-room? No one's going to look there.'

'It's not one hundred per cent safe,' she said. 'Someone could knock the pot over and the soil would spill out on the floor and presto, there's a sparkling diamond lying there.'

'It's a thousand to one against that,' he said. 'It's a thousand to one against the house being broken into anyway.'

'No, it's not,' she said. 'Houses are being burgled every

day. It's not worth chancing it. But look, darling, I'm not going to let this thing become a nuisance to you, or a worry.'

'I agree with that,' he said.

They sipped their drinks for a while in silence.

'I've got it!' she cried, leaping up from her chair. 'I've thought of a marvellous place!'

'Where?'

'In here,' she cried, picking up the ice-tray and pointing to one of the empty compartments. 'We'll just drop it in here and fill it with water and put it back in the fridge. In an hour or two it'll be hidden inside a solid block of ice and even if you looked, you wouldn't be able to see it.'

Robert Sandy stared at the ice-tray. 'It's fantastic!' he said. 'You're a genius! Let's do it right away!'

'Shall we really do it?'

'Of course. It's a terrific idea.'

She picked up the diamond and placed it into one of the little empty compartments. She went to the sink and carefully filled the whole tray with water. She opened the door of the freezer section of the fridge and slid the tray in. 'It's the top tray on the left,' she said. 'We'd better remember that. And it'll be in the block of ice furthest away on the right-hand side of the tray.'

'The top tray on the left,' he said. 'Got it. I feel better now that it's tucked safely away.'

'Finish your drink, darling,' she said. 'Then we must be off. I've packed your case for you. And we'll try not to think about our million pounds any more until we come back.'

'Do we talk about it to other people?' he asked her. 'Like the Renshaws or anyone else who might be there?'

'I wouldn't,' she said. 'It's such an incredible story that it would soon spread around all over the place. Next thing you know, it would be in the papers.'

'I don't think the King of the Saudis would like that,' he said.

'Nor do I. So let's say nothing at the moment.'

'I agree,' he said. 'I would hate any kind of publicity.'

'You'll be able to get yourself a new car,' she said, laughing.

'So I will. I'll get one for you, too. What kind would you like, darling?'

'I'll think about it,' she said.

Soon after that, the two of them drove off to the Renshaws for the weekend. It wasn't far, just beyond Whitney, some thirty minutes from their own house. Charlie Renshaw was a consultant physician at the hospital and the families had known each other for many years.

The weekend was pleasant and uneventful, and on Sunday evening Robert and Betty Sandy drove home again, arriving at the house in Acacia Road at about seven p.m. Robert took the two small suitcases from the car and they walked up the path together. He unlocked the front door and held it open for his wife.

'I'll make some scrambled eggs,' she said, 'and crispy bacon. Would you like a drink first, darling?'

'Why not?' he said.

He closed the door and was about to carry the suitcases

upstairs when he heard a piercing scream from the sitting-room *'Oh no!'* she was crying. *'No! No! No!'*

Robert dropped the suitcase and rushed in after her. She was standing there pressing her hands to her cheeks and already tears were streaming down her face.

The scene in the sitting-room was one of utter desolation. The curtains were drawn and they seemed to be the only things that remained intact in the room. Everything else had been smashed to smithereens. All Robert Sandy's precious little objects from the coffee-table had been picked up and flung against the walls and were lying in tiny pieces on the carpet. A glass cabinet had been tipped over. A chest-of-drawers had had its four drawers pulled out and the contents, photograph albums, games of Scrabble and Monopoly and a chessboard and chessmen and many other family things had been flung across the room. Every single book had been pulled out of the big floor-to-ceiling bookshelves against the far wall and piles of them were now lying open and mutilated all over the place. The glass on each of the four watercolours had been smashed and the oil painting of their three children painted when they were young had had its canvas slashed many times with a knife. The armchairs and the sofa had also been slashed so that the stuffing was bulging out. Virtually everything in the room except the curtains and the carpet had been destroyed.

'Oh, Robert,' she said, collapsing into his arms, 'I don't think I can stand this.'

He didn't say anything. He felt physically sick.

'Stay here,' he said. 'I'm going to look upstairs.' He ran

out and took the stairs two at a time and went first to their bedroom. It was the same in there. The drawers had been pulled out and the shirts and blouses and underclothes were now scattered everywhere. The bedclothes had been stripped from the double-bed and even the mattress had been tipped off the bed and slashed many times with a knife. The cupboards were open and every dress and suit and every pair of trousers and every jacket and every skirt had been ripped from its hanger. He didn't look in the other bedrooms. He ran downstairs and put an arm around his wife's shoulders and together they picked their way through the debris of the sitting-room towards the kitchen. There they stopped.

The mess in the kitchen was indescribable. Almost every single container of any sort in the entire room had been emptied on to the floor and then smashed to pieces. The place was a waste-land of broken jars and bottles and food of every kind. All Betty's home-made jams and pickles and bottled fruits had been swept from the long shelf and lay shattered on the ground. The same had happened to the stuff in the store-cupboard, the mayonnaise, the ketchup, the vinegar, the olive oil, the vegetable oil and all the rest. There were two other long shelves on the far wall and on these had stood about twenty lovely large glass jars with big ground-glass stoppers in which were kept rice and flour and brown sugar and bran and oatmeal and all sorts of other things. Every jar now lay on the floor in many pieces, with the contents spewed around. The refrigerator door was open and the things that had been inside, the leftover foods, the milk, the eggs, the butter, the yoghurt, the tomatoes, the lettuce, all of them had been pulled out and splashed on to the pretty tiled kitchen floor. The inner drawers of the fridge had been thrown into the mass of slush and trampled on. The plastic ice-trays had been yanked out and each had been literally broken in two and thrown aside. Even the plastic-coated shelves had been ripped out of the fridge and bent double and thrown down with the rest. All the bottles of drink, the whisky, gin, vodka, sherry, vermouth, as well as half a dozen cans of beer, were standing on the table, empty. The bottles of drink and the beer cans seemed to be the only things in the entire house that had not been smashed. Practically the whole floor lay under a thick layer of mush and goo. It was as if a gang of mad children had been told to see how much mess they could make and had succeeded brilliantly.

Robert and Betty Sandy stood on the edge of it all, speechless with horror. At last Robert said, 'I imagine our lovely diamond is somewhere underneath all that.'

'I don't give a damn about our diamond,' Betty said. 'I'd like to kill the people who did this.'

'So would I,' Robert said. 'I've got to call the police.' He went back into the sitting-room and picked up the telephone. By some miracle it still worked.

The first squad car arrived in a few minutes. It was followed over the next half-hour by a police inspector, a couple of plain-clothes men, a finger-print expert and a photographer.

The Inspector had a black moustache and a short muscular body. 'These are not professional thieves,' he told Robert Sandy after he had taken a look round. 'They weren't even amateur thieves. They were simply hooligans off the street. Riff-raff. Yobbos. Probably three of them. People like this scout around looking for an empty house and when they find it they break in and the first thing they do is to hunt out the booze. Did you have much alcohol on the premises?'

'The usual stuff,' Robert said. 'Whisky, gin, vodka, sherry and a few cans of beer.'

'They'll have drunk the lot,' the Inspector said. 'Lads like these have only two things in mind, drink and destruction. They collect all the booze on to a table and sit down and drink themselves raving mad. Then they go on the rampage.'

'You mean they didn't come in here to steal?' Robert asked.

'I doubt they've stolen anything at all,' the Inspector said. 'If they'd been thieves they would at least have taken your TV set. Instead, they smashed it up.'

'But why do they do this?'

'You'd better ask their parents,' the Inspector said. 'They're rubbish, that's all they are, just rubbish. People aren't brought up right any more these days.'

Then Robert told the Inspector about the diamond. He gave him all the details from the beginning to end because he realized that from the police point of view it was likely to be the most important part of the whole business.

'Half a million quid!' cried the Inspector. 'Jesus Christ!'

'Probably double that,' Robert said.

'Then that's the first thing we look for,' the Inspector said.

'I personally do not propose to go down on my hands and knees grubbing around in that pile of slush,' Robert said. 'I don't feel like it at this moment.'

'Leave it to us,' the Inspector said. 'We'll find it. That was a clever place to hide it.'

'My wife thought of it. But tell me, Inspector, if by some remote chance they *had* found it . . .'

'Impossible,' the Inspector said. 'How could they?'

'They might have seen it lying on the floor after the ice had melted,' Robert said. 'I agree it's unlikely. But if they *had* spotted it, would they have taken it?'

'I think they would,' the Inspector said. 'No one can resist a diamond. It has a sort of magnetism about it. Yes, if one of them had seen it on the floor, I think he would have slipped it into his pocket. But don't worry about it, doctor. It'll turn up.'

'I'm not worrying about it,' Robert said. 'Right now, I'm worrying about my wife and about our house. My wife spent years trying to make this place into a good home.'

'Now look, sir,' the Inspector said, 'the thing for you to do tonight is to take your wife off to a hotel and get some rest. Come back tomorrow, both of you, and we'll start sorting things out. There'll be someone here all the time looking after the house.'

'I have to operate at the hospital first thing in the morning,' Robert said. 'But I expect my wife will try to come along.'

'Good,' the Inspector said. 'It's a nasty upsetting business having your house ripped apart like this. It's a big shock. I've seen it many times. It hits you very hard.'

Robert and Betty Sandy stayed the night at Oxford's Randolph Hotel, and by eight o'clock the following morning Robert was in the Operating Theatre at the hospital, beginning to work his way through his morning list.

Shortly after noon, Robert had finished his last operation, a straightforward non-malignant prostate on an elderly male. He removed his rubber gloves and mask and went next door to the surgeons' small rest-room for a cup of coffee. But before he got his coffee, he picked up the telephone and called his wife.

'How are you, darling?' he said.

'Oh Robert, it's so *awful*,' she said. 'I just don't know where to begin.'

'Have you called the insurance company?'

'Yes, they're coming any moment to help me make a list.'

'Good,' he said. 'And have the police found our diamond?'

'I'm afraid not,' she said. 'They've been through every bit of that slush in the kitchen and they swear it's not there.'

'Then where can it have gone? Do you think the vandals found it?'

'I suppose they must have,' she said. 'When they broke those ice-trays all the ice-cubes would have fallen out. They fall out when you just bend the tray. They're meant to.'

'They still wouldn't have spotted it in the ice,' Robert said.

'They would when the ice melted,' she said. 'Those

men must have been in the house for hours. Plenty of time for it to melt.'

'I suppose you're right.'

'It would stick out a mile lying there on the floor,' she said, 'the way it shines.'

'Oh dear,' Robert said.

'If we never get it back we won't miss it much anyway, darling,' she said. 'We only had it a few hours.'

'I agree,' he said. 'Do the police have any leads on who the vandals were?'

'Not a clue,' she said. 'They found lots of finger-prints, but they don't seem to belong to any known criminals.'

'They wouldn't,' he said, 'not if they were hooligans off the street.'

'That's what the Inspector said.'

'Look, darling,' he said, 'I've just about finished here for the morning. I'm going to grab some coffee, then I'll come home to give you a hand.'

'Good,' she said. 'I need you, Robert. I need you badly.'

'Just give me five minutes to rest my feet,' he said, 'I feel exhausted.'

In Number Two Operating Theatre not ten yards away, another senior surgeon called Brian Goff was also nearly finished for the morning. He was on his last patient, a young man who had a piece of bone lodged somewhere in his small intestine. Goff was being assisted by a rather jolly young registrar named William Haddock, and between them they had opened the patient's abdomen and Goff was lifting out a section of the small intestine and feeling along it with his fingers. It was routine stuff and there was a good deal of conversation going on in the room.

'Did I ever tell you about the man who had lots of little live fish in his bladder?' William Haddock was saying.

'I don't think you did,' Goff said.

'When we were students at Barts,' William Haddock said, 'we were being taught by a particularly unpleasant Professor of Urology. One day, this twit was going to demonstrate how to examine the bladder using a cystoscope. The patient was an old man suspected of having stones. Well now, in one of the hospital waiting-rooms, there was an aquarium that was full of those tiny little fish, neons they're called, brilliant colours, and one of the students sucked up about twenty of them into a syringe and managed to inject them into the patient's bladder when he was under his pre-med, before he was taken up to Theatre for his cystoscopy.'

'That's disgusting!' the theatre sister cried. 'You can stop right there, Mr Haddock!'

Brian Goff smiled behind his mask and said, 'What happened next?' As he spoke, he had about three feet of the patient's small intestine lying on the green sterile sheet, and he was still feeling along it with his fingers.

'When the Professor got the cystoscope into the bladder and put his eye to it,' William Haddock said, 'he started jumping up and down and shouting with excitement.

' "What is it, sir?" the guilty student asked him. "What do you see?"

'"It's fish!" cried the Professor. "There's hundreds of little fish! They're swimming about!"'

'You made it up,' the theatre sister said. 'It's not true.'

'It most certainly is true,' the Registrar said. 'I looked down the cystoscope myself and saw the fish. And they were actually swimming about.'

'We might have expected a fishy story from a man with a name like Haddock,' Goff said. 'Here we are,' he added. 'Here's this poor chap's trouble. You want to feel it?'

William Haddock took the pale grey piece of intestine between his fingers and pressed. 'Yes,' he said. 'Got it.'

'And if you look just there,' Goff said, instructing him, 'you can see where the bit of bone has punctured the mucosa. It's already inflamed.'

Brian Goff held the section of intestine in the palm of his left hand. The sister handed him a scalpel and he made a small incision. The sister gave him a pair of forceps and Goff probed down among all the slushy matter of the intestine until he found the offending object. He brought it out, held firmly in the forceps, and dropped it into the small stainless-steel bowl the sister was holding. The thing was covered in pale brown gunge.

'That's it,' Goff said. 'You can finish this one for me now, can't you, William. I was meant to be at a meeting downstairs fifteen minutes ago.'

'You go ahead,' William Haddock said. 'I'll close him up.'

The senior surgeon hurried out of the Theatre and the Registrar proceeded to sew up, first the incision in the intestine, then the abdomen itself. The whole thing took no more than a few minutes.

'I'm finished,' he said to the anaesthetist.

The man nodded and removed the mask from the patient's face.

'Thank you, sister,' William Haddock said. 'See you tomorrow.' As he moved away, he picked up from the sister's tray the stainless-steel bowl that contained the gunge-covered brown object. 'Ten to one it's a chicken bone,' he said and he carried it to the sink and began rinsing it under the tap.

'Good God, what's this?' he cried. 'Come and look, sister!'

The sister came over to look. 'It's a piece of costume jewellery,' she said. 'Probably part of a necklace. Now how on earth did he come to swallow that?'

'He'd have passed it if it hadn't had such a sharp point,' William Haddock said. 'I think I'll give it to my girlfriend.'

'You can't do that, Mr Haddock,' the sister said. 'It belongs to the patient. Hang on a sec. Let me look at it again.' She took the stone from William Haddock's gloved hand and carried it into the powerful light that hung over the operating table. The patient had now been lifted off the table and was being wheeled out into Recovery next door, accompanied by the anaesthetist.

'Come here, Mr Haddock,' the sister said, and there was an edge of excitement in her voice. William Haddock joined her under the light. 'This is amazing,' she went on. 'Just look at the way it sparkles and shines. A bit of glass wouldn't do that.'

'Maybe it's rock-crystal,' William Haddock said, 'or topaz, one of those semi-precious stones.'

'You know what I think,' the sister said. 'I think it's a diamond.'

'Don't be damn silly,' William Haddock said.

A junior nurse was wheeling away the instrument trolley and a male theatre assistant was helping to clear up. Neither of them took any notice of the young surgeon and the sister. The sister was about twenty-eight years old, and now that she had removed her mask she appeared as an extremely attractive young lady.

'It's easy enough to test it,' William Haddock said. 'See if it cuts glass.'

Together they crossed over to the frosted-glass window of the operating-room. The sister held the stone between finger and thumb and pressed the sharp pointed end against the glass and drew it downward. There was a fierce scraping crunch as the point bit into the glass and left a deep line two inches long.

'Jesus Christ!' William Haddock said. 'It *is* a diamond!'

'If it is, it belongs to the patient,' the sister said firmly.

'Maybe it does,' William Haddock said, 'but he was mighty glad to get rid of it. Hold on a moment. Where are his notes?' He hurried over to the side table and picked up a folder which said on it JOHN DIGGS. He opened the folder. In it there was an X-ray of the patient's intestine accompanied by the radiologist's report. *John Diggs*, the report said. *Age 17. Address 123 Mayfield Road, Oxford. There is clearly a large obstruction of some sort in the upper small intestine. The patient has no recollection of swallowing anything unusual, but says that he ate some fried chicken on Sunday evening. The object clearly has a sharp point that has pierced the mucosa of the intestine, and it could be a piece of bone . . .*

'How could he swallow a thing like that without knowing it?' William Haddock said.

'It doesn't make sense,' the sister said.

'There's no question it's a diamond after the way it cut the glass,' William Haddock said. 'Do you agree?'

'Absolutely,' the sister said.

'And a bloody big one at that,' Haddock said. 'The question is, how good a diamond is it? How much is it worth?'

'We'd better send it to the lab right away,' the sister said.

'To hell with the lab,' Haddock said. 'Let's have a bit of fun and do it ourselves.'

'How?'

'We'll take it to Gold's, the jeweller's in The High. They'll know. The damn thing must be worth a fortune. We're not going to steal it, but we're damn well going to find out about it. Are you game?'

'Do you know anyone at Gold's?' the sister said.

'No, but that doesn't matter. Do you have a car?'

'My Mini's in the car park.'

'Right. Get changed. I'll meet you out there. It's about your lunch time anyway. I'll take the stone.'

Twenty minutes later, at a quarter to one, the little Mini pulled up outside the jewellery shop of H. F. Gold and parked on the double-yellow lines. 'Who cares,' William Haddock said. 'We won't be long.' He and the sister went into the shop.

There were two customers inside, a young man and a girl. They were examining a tray of rings and were being served by the woman assistant. As soon as they came in, the assistant pressed a bell under the counter and Harry Gold emerged through the door at the back. 'Yes,' he said to William Haddock and the sister. 'Can I help you?'

'Would you mind telling us what this is worth?' William Haddock said, placing the stone on a piece of green cloth that lay on the counter.

Harry Gold stopped dead. He stared at the stone. Then he looked up at the young man and woman who stood before him. He was thinking very fast. Steady now, he told himself. Don't do anything silly. Act natural.

'Well well,' he said as casually as he could. 'That looks to me like a very fine diamond, a very fine diamond indeed. Would you mind waiting a moment while I weigh it and examine it carefully in my office? Then perhaps I'll be able to give you an accurate valuation. Do sit down, both of you.'

Harry Gold scuttled back into his office with the diamond in his hand. Immediately, he took it to the electronic scale and weighed it. Fifteen point two seven carats. That was exactly the weight of Mr Robert Sandy's stone! He had been certain it was the same one the moment he saw it. Who could mistake a diamond like that? And now the weight had proved it. His instinct was to call the police right away, but he was a cautious man who did not like making mistakes. Perhaps the doctor had already sold his diamond. Perhaps he had given it to his children. Who knows?

Quickly he picked up the Oxford telephone book. The

Radcliffe Infirmary was Oxford 249891. He dialled it. He asked for Mr Robert Sandy. He got Robert's secretary. He told her it was most urgent that he speak to Mr Sandy this instant. The secretary said, 'Hold on, please.' She called the Operating Theatre. Mr Sandy had gone home half an hour ago, they told her. She took up the outside phone and relayed this information to Mr Gold.

'What's his home number?' Mr Gold asked her.

'Is this to do with a patient?'

'No!' cried Harry Gold. 'It's to do with a robbery! For heaven's sake, woman, give me that number quickly!'

'Who is speaking, please?'

'Harry Gold! I'm the jeweller in The High! Don't waste time, I beg you!'

She gave him the number.

Harry Gold dialled again.

'Mr Sandy?'

'Speaking.'

'This is Harry Gold, Mr Sandy, the jeweller. Have you by any chance lost your diamond?'

'Yes, I have.'

'Two people have just brought it into my shop,' Harry Gold whispered excitedly. 'A man and a woman. Youngish. They're trying to get it valued. They're waiting out there now.'

'Are you certain it's my stone?'

'Positive. I weighed it.'

'Keep them there, Mr Gold!' Robert Sandy cried. 'Talk to them! Humour them! Do anything! I'm calling the police!'

Robert Sandy called the police station. Within seconds, he was giving the news to the Detective Inspector who was in charge of the case. 'Get there fast and you'll catch them both!' he said. 'I'm on my way, too!'

'Come on, darling!' he shouted to his wife. 'Jump in the car. I think they've found our diamond and the thieves are in Harry Gold's shop right now trying to sell it!'

When Robert and Betty Sandy drove up to Harry Gold's shop nine minutes later, two police cars were already parked outside. 'Come on, darling,' Robert said. 'Let's go in and see what's happening.'

There was a good deal of activity inside the shop when Robert and Betty Sandy rushed in. Two policemen and two plain-clothes detectives, one of them the Inspector, were surrounding a furious William Haddock and an even more furious theatre sister. Both the young surgeon and the theatre sister were handcuffed.

'You found it *where*?' the Inspector was saying.

'Take these damn handcuffs off me!' the sister was shouting. 'How dare you do this!'

'Tell us again where you found it,' the Inspector said, caustic.

'In someone's stomach!' William Haddock yelled back at him. 'I've told you twice!'

'Don't give me that crap!' the Inspector said.

'Good God, William!' Robert Sandy cried as he came in and saw who it was. 'And Sister Wyman! What on earth are you two doing here?'

'They had the diamond,' the Inspector said. 'They were trying to flog it. Do you know these people, Mr Sandy?'

It didn't take very long for William Haddock to explain to Robert Sandy, and indeed to the Inspector, exactly how and where the diamond had been found.

'Remove their handcuffs, for heaven's sake, Inspector,' Robert Sandy said. 'They're telling the truth. The man you want, at least one of the men you want, is in the hospital right now, just coming round from his anaesthetic. Isn't that right, William?'

'Correct,' William Haddock said. 'His name is John Diggs. He'll be in one of the surgical wards.'

Harry Gold stepped forwards. 'Here's your diamond, Mr Sandy,' he said.

'Now listen,' the theatre sister said, still angry, 'would someone for God's sake tell me how that patient came to swallow a diamond like this without knowing he'd done it?'

'I think I can guess,' Robert Sandy said. 'He allowed himself the luxury of putting ice in his drink. Then he got very drunk. Then he swallowed a piece of half-melted ice.'

'I still don't get it,' the sister said.

'I'll tell you the rest later,' Robert Sandy said. 'In fact, why don't we all go round the corner and have a drink ourselves.'

Princess Mammalia

First published in *Two Fables* (1986)

When Princess Mammalia arose from her bed on the morning of her seventeenth birthday and examined her face in the looking-glass, she couldn't believe what she saw. Up until then she had always been a rather plain and dumpy girl with a thick neck, but now she suddenly found herself staring at a young lady she had never set eyes on before. A magical transformation had taken place overnight and the dumpy little Princess had become a dazzling beauty. I use the word 'dazzling' in its purest and most literal sense, for such a blaze of glory, such a scintillation of stars, such a blinding beauty shone forth from her countenance that when she went downstairs an hour later to open her presents, those who gazed upon her at close quarters had to screw up their eyes for fear the brilliance of it all might damage their retinas. Even the royal astronomer was heard to murmur that it might be safer to view the lady through smoked glass, as one would the eclipse of the sun.

Ever since she had learned to walk, Princess Mammalia had been much loved around the Palace for her modest and gentle disposition, but she very soon found out that it is much more difficult for a ravishing beauty to remain modest and gentle than it is for a plain girl. She discovered that the kind of extraordinary beauty she possessed endowed her with immense power. In the glittering presence of her new-found image, men became so overwhelmed with desire that they were hers to command. Caliphs and rajas, grand viziers and generals, ministers and chancellors, camel drivers and rent collectors, all of them melted into a froth as soon as she appeared on the scene. They fawned and simpered. They drooled and dribbled. They crawled and toadied. She had only to lift her little finger and they all started scampering around the room in their efforts to please her. They offered her rich jewels and golden bracelets. They suggested lavish feasts in cool places, and whenever one of them got her in a corner on her own, he began to whisper obscenities in her ear. There were also problems with the staff. A servant is just as much of a man as a courtier, and after several unsavoury incidents in the corridors, the King was forced, much against his wishes, for he was a kind king, to order that all male servants in the Palace be castrated immediately. Only the royal chef escaped. He pleaded that it would ruin his cooking.

At first, and with charming innocence, the Princess simply sat back and enjoyed her new-found power. But that couldn't go on. Nobody, let alone a maiden of seventeen, could remain unaffected for long. This was power indeed. It was power unheard of in one so young. And power itself, the Princess soon discovered, is a demanding taskmaster. It is impossible to have it and not use it. It insists on being exercised. Thus the Princess began consciously to exercise her power over men, first in small ways, then in rather bigger ones. It was ridiculously easy, like manipulating puppets.

At this point, the Princess made her second discovery, and it was this. If the power of a female is so great that men will obey her without question, she becomes contemptuous of those men, and within a month, the Princess found that the only feelings she had towards the male species were those of scorn and contumely. She began to practise all manner of droll stratagems to humiliate her worshippers. She took, for example, to going on walkabouts in the city and displaying herself to ordinary men in the street. Surrounded by her faithful guard of eunuchs, she would watch with amusement as the male citizens went crazy with desire at the sight of her blazing beauty, hurling themselves against the spears of the guards and becoming impaled by the hundreds.

Late at night, before retiring to bed, she would divert herself by strolling out on to her balcony and showing herself to the lascivious *polloi* who were wont to gather in their thousands in the courtyard below, hoping for a glimpse of her. And why not indeed? She looked more dazzling and desirable than ever standing there in the moonlight. In truth, she outshone the moon itself, and the citizens would go berserk as soon as she appeared, crying out and tearing their hair and fracturing their bones by flinging themselves against the craggy walls of the Palace. Every now and again, the Princess would pour a pipkin or two of boiling lead over their heads to cool them down.

All this was bad enough, but there was worse to come. As we all know, power, with all its subtle facets, is a voracious bedfellow. The more one has, the more one wants. There is no such thing as getting enough of it, and over the next few months the Princess's craving for power grew and grew until in the end she found herself beginning to toy with the idea of gaining for herself the ultimate power in the land, the throne itself.

She was the eldest of seven children, all of them girls, and her mother was dead. Already, therefore, she was the rightful heir to her father's throne. But what good was that? Her father, the King, who not so long ago had been the idol of her eye, now irritated her to distraction. He was a benign and merciful ruler, much loved by his people, and because he was her father he was the only man in the Kingdom who did not turn cartwheels at the sight of her. What was worse, he was in excellent health.

Such is the terrible corrupting influence of power that the young Princess now began actually to plot the destruction of her own father. But that was easier said than done. It is extremely difficult to bump off a great ruler all on your own without being caught. Poison was a possibility, but poisoners are nearly always apprehended. She spent many days and nights ruminating upon this problem, but no answer came to her. Then one evening after supper, she strolled out on to her balcony as usual, thinking to divert herself for a few moments by driving the crowd of lecherous citizens crazy but, lo and behold, on this night there was no crowd. Instead, an old beggerman stood alone in the courtyard, gazing up at her. He was dressed in filthy rags and his feet were bare. He had a long white beard and a mane of snow-white hair that reached to his shoulders, and he leaned heavily upon a stick.

'Go away, you disgusting old man,' she called out.

'Ssshh!' the old beggar whispered, edging closer. 'I am here to help you. It has come to me in a vision that you are deeply troubled.'

'I am not in the least troubled,' the Princess answered. 'Be off with you unless you fancy a pipkin of boiling lead over your noddle.'

The old man ignored her. 'There is only one way in the world,' he whispered, 'to dispose of an enemy without being caught. Do you wish to hear it?'

'Certainly not,' the Princess snapped. 'Why should I? Yes, what is it?'

'You take an oyster,' the old man whispered, 'and you bury it in the soil of a potted plant. Twenty-four hours later, you dig it up and you squeeze one droplet of its juice, just one droplet, mind you, on to each of the oysters that you are serving to the victim on the following day.'

'Does that fix him?' the Princess asked, unable to conceal her interest.

'It is lethal,' whispered the old man. 'The person who eats those oysters will succumb very swiftly to a terrible paroxysm that will tie his whole body into knots. And after it is over, the whole world will simply shake their heads and murmur, "Poor fellow, he ate a very bad oyster."'

'Who are you, old man, and where do you come from?' the Princess asked, leaning over the balcony.

'I am on the side of the righteous,' the old man whispered, and with that he disappeared into the shadows.

The Princess stored this information away in her head and patiently bided her time. A few days before her eighteenth birthday, the King said to her, 'What do you want for your birthday dinner, my dear? Shall it be your favourite roast boar as usual?'

'Yes, papa,' she answered. 'But let us have some oysters first. I do so love oysters.'

'What a capital idea,' answered the King. 'I shall send to the coast for them immediately.'

On the Princess's birthday, the table in the great dining-room was sumptuously laid and all was got ready for the feast. One dozen fine oysters were put in each place, but before the guests went in to take their seats, the King entered the room alone, as was his wont on special occasions, to make sure that all was to his liking. He summoned the butler and together the two of them walked slowly round the table.

'Why,' asked the King, pointing to his own plate, 'have you given to me the biggest and choicest oysters?'

'Your Majesty always receives the best of everything,' replied the butler, speaking in a high voice. 'Have I done wrong?'

'Today the Princess Mammalia must have the best,' the King said. 'She is the birthday girl. So kindly give her my plate and give me hers.'

'At once, Your Majesty,' answered the butler, and he hastened to change the plates round.

The birthday feast was a success and the oysters went down particularly well. 'Do you like them, Papa?' Princess Mammalia kept asking her father. 'Are they not succulent?'

'Mine are delicious,' the King said. 'How are yours?'

'Perfect,' she answered. 'They are just perfect.'

That night Princess Mammalia was taken violently ill,

and despite the ministrations of the royal physician, she succumbed to a terrible paroxysm that tied her beautiful body into knots.

The next morning the King took from his closet the long white false beard, the long white wig, the filthy rags and the old walking-stick. 'You can burn these,' he said to his valet. 'We can't have fancy-dress parties while the court is in mourning.'

We believe in doing good things.

That's why ten per cent of all Roald Dahl income* goes to our charity partners. We have supported causes including: specialist children's nurses, grants for families in need, and educational outreach programmes. Thank you for helping us to sustain this vital work.

Find out more at roalddahl.com

ROALD DAHL

Roald Dahl was a spy, ace fighter pilot, chocolate historian and medical inventor. He was also the author of *Charlie and the Chocolate Factory*, *Matilda*, *The BFG* and many more brilliant stories. He remains the World's No.1 storyteller.